# HAWK

**WILLIAM WALLIS**

Stone & Scott, *Publishers*

©2006 by William George Wallis

All rights reserved. No part of this book may be reproduced, transmitted, or performed in any manner without written permission from the publisher except for brief passages in reviews or critical studies.

Library of Congress Cataloging-in-Publication Data
Wallis, William George, 1946-
  Hawk: a novel / William Wallis.–1st ed.
    p. cm.
  ISBN-13: 978-1-891135-07-1
  1. Boys–Fiction.  2. Arkansas–Fiction.  3. Rural families–Fiction.
4. Abused children–Fiction.  5. Loss (Psychology)–Fiction.  6. Children with visual disabilities  7. Race relations–Fiction.  I. Title.

PS3573.A4386H39 2005
813'.54–dc22
                            2005024452

Stone and Scott, *Publishers*
P.O. Box 56419
Sherman Oaks, CA 91413-1419
www.stoneandscott.com

Printed in the United States of America by
Delta Printing Solutions, Valencia, CA

*Designed by Lynn Eames*

For Shawn —

All good wishes —

Bill
October 2005

# HAWK

**WILLIAM WALLIS**

*For*
*David Landis*

## Falke Family Chronology

| | |
|---|---|
| 1866 | Walter Wallis Falke born, Trigg County, Kentucky |
| 1878 | Elizabeth Grace Parker, first wife of Walter, born Trigg County |
| 1882 | Penecia "Nici" Jane Parker, second wife of Walter, born Trigg County |
| 1900 | Walter marries Elizabeth in Cadiz |
| 1901 | Lennie Falke is born, Trigg County |
| 1902 | Faye Falke is born, Trigg County |
| 1904 | Elizabeth dies of "pneumonia" |
| 1905 | Walter marries Penecia Parker |
| 1906 | Ray "Ted" Falke is born, Trigg County |
| 1909 | Faye dies of infection |
| 1910 | Penecia dies of tuberculosis |
| 1914 | Ruth Jeanne Crooks is born, Lorraine, Ohio |
| 1930 | Walter dies of infection, Trigg County |
| 1939 | Ray marries Ruth, West Palm Beach, Florida |
| 1941 | Barbara Falke is born, West Palm Beach |
| 1942 | Frederick Ray Falke is born, dies three days later from "pneumonia" |
| 1944 | Judith Kay Falke is born |
| 1946 | William "Will" Falke is born, Eustis, Florida |
| 1948 | Flora Poenicia "Nici" Falke is born, Elberton, Georgia |
| 1949 | The Falkes move to Monticello, Arkansas |

In June 1951, the Falke family moved from Lake Shore Drive, College Heights/Monticello, Arkansas, to a farm one mile southwest of Arkansas Agricultural and Mechanical College, where Ray Falke taught Industrial Education. His children attended nearby Drew Central Schools. When the Falkes moved north to Pine Bluff in 1959, Ray Falke was remembered as a gentleman farmer, an industrious worker, and an eloquent public speaker. His neighbors remembered him as the man who in 1955 brought running water to their community.

"O cricket is to cricket dear, and ant for
      ant doth long,
The hawk's the darling of his fere, and
      o' me the Muse and her song."

—Theocritus, 3rd c. BC
*The Third Country Singing Match*


"Whoo-oop! I'm the old original iron-jawed, brass-mounted, copper-bellied corpse-maker from the wilds of Arkansaw. Look at me! I'm the man they call Sudden Death and General Desolation! ...."

—Samuel Clemens
*The Adventures of Huckleberry Finn*


"Well, that's infernal mean. Odd, too. Say, boy, what's the matter with your father?"

—Clemens, *Ibid.*


"In this last conflict, however, there had been some minutes of the supreme fire of the hawk whose three hungers are perfectly fused in the one will; enough to burn off a year of shame."

—Walter Van Tilburg Clark
*Hook*

# HAWK

## WILLIAM WALLIS

## *Prelude*

That early spring, near the end of the first year on the farm, Will often stood at sunset, after chores—among the small cluster of ramshackle buildings that served as a shelter to their farm animals—and looked southwest over the rolling powder pastures of south Arkansas. Beyond the old creek bed, he saw the low-lying cloud of blackberry briars, grey thorns, and weeds hovering along the levee of the old pond a quarter mile away. To its right stood the great pine. As he sifted the dust of the barnyard between his toes, he imagined the mud that sucked deeply at his feet near the pond's edge. Last July, the brackish water had withdrawn, leaving a web of cracks that ran away toward the woods from the slow boiling rim of slimy mud, and he gripped the edges of the fissures with his bare toes and crouching, dreamed of slipping down into the earth.

During that first year, Will explored the farm's fifty acres with a growing knowledge of the forces hidden in the rough landscape. As fall's chill ran through the fields and forests, the landscape slipped off its bright layers of leaves, and he found it necessary to put layers of clothing on, even to wear socks and shoes. The autumn and winter following their summer move to the farm were dry, and, in this first spring, the pale brush and trees hardened in the early stages of drought. He brushed the brittle tops of the minute pine sprouts that his father and he had planted on cool September and cold October weekends.

Will ranged over the land, at first fitfully exploring along the rickety barbed wire fences that marked its boundaries, and then in rough geometric patterns he called patches, after something in a story his maiden aunt read to him one summer in Hopkinsville. He divided the acreage into these patches and imagined it a great quilt, like one his aunt sewed with her friends on long summer evenings in Kentucky. That first year Will explored the swath of oak woods to the west and south of the central pastures that ran to the southeast in slight rolling slopes. He watched the gradual shifts in color of the things that grew, he delighted in the sounds and mimicked the animals wild and tame, and he watched clouds being shaped by the invisible force of the wind. Gradually, the farm became his.

In fall afternoons that first year, he sometimes worked alone clearing brush near the pond. That ceased in winter, because it *was nearly dark when he arrived home from school. Then, the clearing continued in spring, when the days grew longer. His hatchet cut young oak and hickory scrub, and he gathered the unwanted branches. At four-thirty, like clockwork, a pair of huge cows swayed down the dusty path to the pond, plunged into the dark green water and sucked it inside the stomachs that swelled their barrel ribs. When he approached them, they thrust their broad, smooth black noses into his empty hands, leaving cool indentures on his palms. He rubbed the shiny moisture on the dry grass where broken stalks had lain under snow and ice two months before. He shivered at the thought.*

*Then, like a sign, his father—tools gathered on his shoulder—strode down from the shed past the barn, long steps swimming in the late afternoon heat. He called and raised his free arm, signaling his son to meet him at the dry creek bed between them. Will ran toward his father's great strides, uncaring as the acorns and twigs stabbed his feet; he tore down into the creek bed and emerged in front of his father. Then they crossed the dry ditch together, in the son's slender arms the unwieldy hoe, across his father's shoulder the double-edged axe.*

*They entered the woods together to cut and clear brush and the undergrowth it hid. The boy worked and sweated near his father. His hands and arms were dirty, then grimy, then caked with dusty mud, leaves, and traces of bark. His father's axe whistled close to the boy's head and thudded into the brush roots. Tiny fragments of leaf and bark filled the sunny air about him, like fireflies. There was salt water in his mouth and dripping from his nose—cross-eyed boy. The hours slipped away into action, the war of men with nature. Nearby, the great pine towered over the oak forests and drew his eye.*

*When the sun sat on the second branch of his pine, Will, his father, and their long shadows rippled up to the house and to mother and sisters for supper. He washed his hands at the cistern in the back yard near the large fig tree that burst from beside the feed house into the yard like pale green fire on July fourth. In the early evening light, the water was cold and sweet, almost a metallic thing in its sweeping arc from the bucket tipping at the cistern's edge to the thick rye grass of the lawn below, broken only by his mouth's sucking thirst.*

*Then to the table where strict rules abided.* We raise this food ourselves, *said his father proudly from the end of the table. Will sat quietly humming to himself while the family buzzed around him. His sisters always fought. There was never enough food to fill his emptiness. There was never enough of his mother's touch.*

*After a slender slice of apple pie, he went to the darkness of his room, where sinewy panthers played in the shadows at the foot of his bed for endless moments. Gradually, stroking the rough, fragrant cotton of the pillowcase, he sighed the dreaming sigh and drifted down through his pillow to the pond again. Insects seethed and murmured in masses within and above the water's surface; they preyed upon one another while the ancient body sang from its depths of the mysteries of wetness and warmth.*

*And nearby, close to the center of the property, stood the great pine, a perch for the boy on stormy days and an axis for the circling flight of his Hawk.*

## PART ONE
### Spring 1952

Our first days together I sang victories
Unknown from your shoulder, clutching rough
Cheeks, tufts of weather-beaten, iron hair—
Once you were a moment blind with hand hugs.
I danced before the high wagon you drove out
To autumn planting and, crouching wet kneed,
We tufted the empty pastures with pine sprouts.
Reedy music bent us both under airy gray crowns.
Later, my endless search for love in progress,
These eyes studied feral horizons for answers
You had uttered in restless voice, now an echo
Spinning in my worded room these warmer years.
Old Dad, after love ends the dance of fear,
Allow your son to revere lost elegance.

## ONE

*Arc-and-saw*, as Will liked to say it, was named after a river that flowed from the northwest and wandered down across that rough square of green and gold that was bound to the east by the dark blue squirm of the Mississippi. That first winter on the farm, Will tacked that old map to the naked sheet rock serving as the west wall of his room. Will's room was on the south side of the house between his parent's bedroom and his sisters' room, which filled the southwest corner. A narrow hallway ran from his parents' bedroom past the bathroom, his room, and then doglegged right into the kitchen. The single small bathroom separated Will's room from the mysteries of his parents' bedroom, which was very quiet except for his father's snoring. His two older sisters' room was, however, anything but quiet. They argued constantly. Little Poenicia—Nici, to Will—was four and had her own small bed within her older sisters' room. Will pitied her the sleeping arrangement, but Nici's was the gift of deep and untroubled sleep.

Months before, beginning in September, Will and his father began replacing every ceiling, wall, and floor of that house, one board at a time. That work filled most weekend afternoons and evenings, and every holiday. The south side of the house was in constant disrepair during that early spring, and the hallway was sometimes filled with tools, sacks of nails, and various building materials. The old floor was still there, but the hallway ceiling and walls and Will's room were gutted and being replaced as his father found money for materials. The finishing work and the flooring would go on at a snail's pace for the next two years, so slowly that by the time a room was finished, it was not something Will could truly measure. There was no wonder in it. It was simply the end of one task that preceded the next. *Work is never done on a farm*, Will's father, Ray, often said grimly, as he drove in a sixteen-penny nail with three clean strokes or dug a hole for a fence post.

The boy was restless at the many tasks he was given by his father. He helped with the daily chores; he worked the fields, fed the animals—chickens, one pig, and the horse, Lady—and milked the two cows. He was at first hurt by the anger in his father. He understood that things were sometimes not right, not as his father wanted them to be, and that his father needed his help in fixing them. Will, in most ways like his gentle mother, was hurt when his dreaming or soft singing caused his father to bark out at him like a huge dog.

He began to see that his father and mother were very different kinds of people. There were those who brought pain to others, like his father, and there were people to whom pain seemed attracted, like his mother and him. While his father could be fascinated by the craftsmanship of those who built the house and such details as the square nails he pulled from the rotting pine boards of the living room walls, Will saw clearly that his mother found no such pleasure in the details of rebuilding the house. She yearned for something else, something vague and distant. Will tried to imagine it. Perhaps it was a beautiful place she knew when she was a girl. Will began to think about the house and his mother at the same time, as if he was working on it for her. This made the work easier.

Will was at home with physical pain, lived with it in his eye, day and night. And there were the trips to the stump—that was shocking pain, yet he accustomed himself to that as well. There were also jumps from the garage roof, falls from trees and horses, and sometimes brief, violent struggles with boys at school. Then there were words. He was shocked at the power of words to cause a kind of pain very different from the sharp, deep itch in his eye or the sting of the razor strap. This other kind of pain was terrible. Sometimes it seemed to him as if they—he and his mother—had been tainted from birth by knowledge of a place apart from the others surrounding them, a place of quiet and peace, dream-like. He called this world *the beside place*. He could go there, not whenever he wished, but often enough for comfort. He went there by losing himself in certain places he hunted out—mostly on the farm, though one important one was over a mile away, on the campus where his father taught—and lingering there in a kind of waking dream. He found enough special places and learned to think in certain ways, and so he survived the years after he returned from the hospital in Little Rock. He was beginning the third of those years.

## TWO

Will did not learn to be as cruel as the thorns or as dry as the fields, but he learned to run and jump like a hare, climb trees like a squirrel, and cling to branches like a wingless bird—even in the strongest wind, even when it seemed that the top of the tree where he perched might break and go flying in the dark stretches of wind. He grew to love the violence of nature, its flooding currents, acrid lightning, and deafening thunder. He also grew less sensitive to cuts and burns and the other irritations of rural life that distracted his sisters. He loved to go barefoot and gladly paid the price for the pleasure. The ringworm circling above his left ankle bothered him only when he had to wear socks and shoes, which he had to for school.

He enjoyed second grade, but it meant wearing shoes. Schoolwork was simple for him; he seemed to recognize the letters and numbers—and the patterns they formed—as something that had always been there, inside him. He scribbled all his homework in study hall, during recess, or on the bus ride home. School was about numbers and words. Numbers were easy, but words were hard to hold, slippery like fish—even when he had them in his hand, they were free to cut him or break away, fall back where they came from.

He had started to read after returning from the hospital when he was four and loved to surround himself with books at the Monticello library on Saturdays when his parents went shopping. Some words took his breath away with pleasure, but he dreaded the white heat people's words sometimes filled him with. In the hospital, he felt a cold dread at the doctors and nurses' words. In the library, the sounds and words of others sometimes paralyzed him. People called him things in a way, with a strange gesture of the eyes or mouths, things that made him shrink or cry, run away to one of his secret places. The power of words was mysterious.

Will felt alone on the farm and found in aloneness a kind of freedom. All their previous houses had been in rows, and their neighbors flowed in and out of open doors. He knew their names, their cars, and their work: they *did* this or that, people said. But the old farmhouse was different. It sat alone on the west side of the gravel road about a mile from the campus where his father taught. Dust rose from the road and coated everything nearby, even on still days.

Right after they moved to the farm, Will began exploring the area where large oak trees stood before and beside the house. In early spring, when Will jumped down from the school bus steps into the the large triangle of weeds that amounted to a front yard area, he took his books to the front porch, then lay under one of the oaks for the brief hour before he had to begin chores. There, lying in the dusty weeds under the oaks, he watched the infrequently traveled rural road. He studied the green and gray Ford trucks that chugged by, loaded with wood, fencing materials, or seed; he watched the clouds of dust that swirled behind every vehicle; and he listened to their music, the tick-tick-tick and whine of engines.

On those Saturdays when he did not go into Monticello to the town library or to see a matinee for two coke bottles, Will became invisible as he lay in the dust near the busy road. For hours, he would lie unnoticed to anyone who walked by. He learned about how painful little things in the dust could be: He made the acquaintance of the small brown scorpions that shuttled like little machines through the thin carpet of dust near the oaks. Above him, squirrels played and dropped large acorns on his shorn, sunburned head. He once saw an escaped canary pecked to death by a large blue jay. He was stung by every kind of insect and became skilled at crushing them before they could extract themselves and escape. He sometimes sat and scratched painful words in the roadside dust.

## THREE

The distance from the white house at the end of Lakeshore Drive to the farm was not great, perhaps two miles—it took only fifteen minutes in the rickety truck Ray Falke borrowed to move his family—but it changed everything for Will, his three sisters, and especially his mother. The farmhouse, which was hastily built from cheap lumber late in the nineteenth century, was a nightmare for Ruth. She experienced it as a retreat to the most primitive aspects of her urban girlhood. It became a struggle that she accepted, but she yearned for better. Slender and pale, she longed for a lyric existence—simpler, clearer. She had no use for complexity, yet she knew that she had chosen a complex man. No matter, for she knew he loved her. And she sang throughout the day for that.

The house had no running water, only a cistern in the back yard. Rusty pipes ran from the sink in the kitchen and the single toilet to a crude septic tank. The wiring concealed behind the fading, curled layers of wallpaper was rudimentary. The wide pine boards that approximated a floor groaned, and the flaking linoleum in the kitchen and bathrooms shifted uneasily beneath her feet. Dust—dust of the road, dust of the fields, dust of the old house itself—appeared on the surface of her kitchen table and her armoire. Like manna, it longed to be gathered up in morning light. The house dust was different from the dust of the road and the fields; it was pungent with mildew and decay. It consisted of tiny bits of paper and wood that smelled of stale, hard times and desolation. Ruth dusted every day and waited for those rotting walls to be gradually transformed from the roof down and the floor joists up by her engineer husband, who remained true to his word to transform the house into a thing of solid beauty.

She fed her family from the gas stove and she fashioned clothes for her daughters on the old Singer sewing machine her mother gave her. She transformed the rough cotton she bought at the store in Monticello or rescued from the chicken feed sacks purchased monthly into loose dresses for her daughters and herself. For Easter, she purchased special fabric, silks and taffetas, and fitted them lovingly around her daughters' changing bodies, so that their restless spirits longed for church, even if choir robes covered their new dresses during services. From time to time, she made work shirts for her husband or for Will.

Her efforts matched her husband's. As she worked, she watched Ray—evenings and weekends, day in and day out—re-roof, tear out the dry filth of the ceilings and walls, put siding on the outside of the house, insert asbestos insulation, and replace the interior walls with sheetrock. He fitted window after window in and laid down fine oak floors. As she watched Ray tear down and rebuild, she sensed a change in him, a furious wrestling she could not yet distinguish from the powerful ambition she admired. She had married a driven man, one very different from her gentle father.

In the years before running water came, Ruth rose early, dusted and cooked, and faithfully raised her children within the rough family circle she and her husband devised as best they could. She scrubbed and fell heavily on that linoleum. She lost much that was precious in that country house, yet gained something that no man or book could truly describe.

### FOUR

For Ray, the farm offered a way to repair his life. This was the piece of land he always wanted to own. Like most men of his time, he rarely considered his wife's perspective. When he promised to recast the house for Ruth, he never saw that the house he mastered had already made her its slave with its creaking, drafts, and shifting dust. Ray's thoughts were mostly practical. He longed to educate his son in the discipline of craft and was certain that the farm was a good place to do it. He taught his boy how to build sturdy structures to shelter family and livestock and how to plant crops to feed them. He saw no special abilities in his Will; he saw him as a dreamer who would never amount to much. This was a world of engineers and the machines they designed, not for dreamers. The 1930s taught him that! Will would learn the necessary skills, whether he wanted to or not. It was the way things were.

Shortly after moving to the farm, Ray dreamed of the house as he wanted it to be. In his dream, the roof of the house swirled lyrically, like deep snow shaped by the winter wind. It was like the roofs of some of the German houses he saw in Ohio during the 1940s, when he was working with Sikorsky. Images of a poem he had memorized in school returned to him, something about leaves swirling in a gust, about snow being carved by wind. *That was long ago*, a voice in the dream said.

It was a modest house, made of solid materials and with trim decorations. It did not call attention to itself, yet beneath its curiously changing crown it was beautiful in its simplicity. Its smooth wood was white, pure. A gable indicated an attic for storage. A modest porch graced its front, with a generous cord of firewood on either side. The doorway was properly screened, but the door stood open, welcoming him. Bright blue curtains peeked from the windows. There was something sweet, even inviting about them. In his dream, he smiled and approached the house, knowing that it was his and that it welcomed him.

When he entered the dream house, he flew from room to room, admiring the rich colors of the solid walls and arching hallways. Curtains billowed in, full of fresh breeze, fragrant with flowers and sun. He was truly happy.

One spring Sunday, Ray awoke startled by tears in his eyes. Ruth was sleeping peacefully beside him. The sun was just coloring the horizon outside his window. He had overslept. Just this once, he said, it was fine. He turned to his wife, his dream still awake within him.

### FIVE

Will's mother was his first storyteller. She read or simply recounted her stories in a lilting voice. Sometimes she sang with a warm sweetness he thrilled to. His favorite song was about a gypsy child and a bird that flew away. The songs were like dreams, but her stories were different. Sometimes when she was tired in the late afternoon, she spoke to him of herself. Each story began with, *Oh, Will, you should have seen....* Of all his mother's stories, he remembered one most clearly. One afternoon just after Will returned from Little Rock, they were sitting on the front steps. Nici slept in her arms. She seemed sad and gazed into the distance as if searching for something.

When his mother was a girl, eight years old, she watched a large truck emerge from the shadowed trees along the road running by their house in West Palm Beach. She daydreamed as her little brother, Buddy, who was four, ran from her side, across the sunlit stretch of lawn, and down into the shadowy ditch before bursting onto the dirt road where he saw his father striding toward him. As in a terrible dream, Ruth watched her little brother, four, run over and crushed up in the wheel well of the enormous machine. Will imagined that the boy's eyes caught his father's a moment before the truck was on him.

Ruth remembered being frozen to the spot, defined in her memory by a soft blue blanket where she and her brother had lain watching insects in the thick grass. As the truck's brakes screeched and its engine sputtered, the entire mechanism lurched to a halt, a grotesque monster that had stumbled. Her father ran forward and bent down to hold the pale little hand that hung out from above the wheel well of the truck. Buddy's slender hand jerked slightly in her kneeling father's hands. Her father was murmuring something that she could not hear. She remembered sensing her mother beside her and was struck by her mother's eyes as they turned to her, terrible with incomprehension and pain.

*What did Daddy say to Buddy?* Ruth moaned to Will.

She told Will this story only once, as she rocked Nici roughly in her arms. He sat still, listening, holding her hand, his own pain disappearing into hers. He remembered every word.

It seemed to Will that most people knew stories, and many enjoyed telling them. He began to seek storytellers out because if he stayed home, he seldom saw folk, even the neighbors. His most favorite was Mr. Chambers, who owned the large farm a quarter-mile south. He was skinny as a rail and told good stories, mostly about planting and growing things. When Will first sought him out, the old farmer seemed to scowl whenever he saw the boy approaching. Will almost ran off the first time he saw that mask but somehow sensed the old man's expression was a wry smile. Will quickly grew accustomed to Mr. Chambers, who gladly told jokes or stories as they walked out to harvest persimmons or pears. Then there was Mr. Gold, from the library, with his quaint stories of lost little boys in a faraway land. His sad, slow smile was so very, very different from Mr. Chambers' cheerful grimace.

## SIX

Will was half blind. Just before his fourth birthday, he tagged along with a group of neighborhood kids into the woods behind the forestry park, about a mile back from Campus Drive, where they lived at the time. At first, all the older kids yelled at him when he wanted to go with them. Later, they ignored him as he willfully followed them into the woods. Several were Cub Scouts, proud of their uniforms. At the park, they reluctantly included him in their procession through the brush that crowded much of the floor beneath the tall pine roof.

When a branch of grey thorns clung to the scout in front of him and then lashed across his face, Will felt a sharp stinging pain in his eye. He cried out. He could no longer see clearly and began to stumble. The group quickly tired of that and the boy behind him started to push him. When Will started to fall, the boy jerked him up like a puppet, again and again. Annoyed at being held back on their hike, the older children teased him. When he fell in a clearing and rolled into a ball, they struck and kicked him. Finally, they left him there in the pine forest, rubbing the fierce itch in his eye and lost in a blurred world so clear to him moments before.

He did not know how long he lay under the trees, but his mother found him there, somehow, and carried him back to the house. Probably one of his older sisters ran the mile back to the house on Campus Drive and fetched her.

Then came the real nightmare, a year of eye operations in Little Rock, a hundred miles away. During that year, he did not see his mother, who had his two-year-old sister Nici to care for. There was also the casual insensitivity and teasing of all but one of the nurses. That nurse, Alma, saved him, with her reading and songs, with her touch. He never saw her, only imagined her from her voice and gentle hands. Once he heard her speaking softly to his father before he came in to visit Will, and on that day his father was unusually warm.

Worse in some ways than the operations themselves were the ether dreams that lingered interminably so that in his blindness—both eyes were covered for almost the entire year in the hospital—he couldn't distinguish between waking and sleeping for long periods of time. The operations occurred during the nine months beginning in August 1950, when Will was three and a half, and ended in early spring the following year. After he returned, the bi-weekly penicillin shots began.

By spring 1952, early in his seventh year, he began to forget some details of the hospital confinement, but for several years he often woke screaming into the dark void of his room. And, as his eye slowly became accustomed to light, he could see the anguished blur of one or both of his parents holding him down on his sweat soaked bed. Sometimes he thought of their exhausted faces in waking moments when he was alone, and he loved them fiercely for being there when he escaped from the hell of his dreams.

Waking pain was another problem entirely. Before he became accustomed to the constant burning in his eye, he thought of it as a snarling dog that gnawed and gnawed, never settled—yelping and snarling at the light. The dog never left him, so it became a fact of life, like wasps and the razor strap—always there, a cool dread.

During the year after he returned from the operations, he clung to his mother so intensely that she feared for him. He was barely four when he returned, but was almost infantile in his longing for her. At the same time, he seemed more mature—still, reserved—than a much older child when she glimpsed him alone or among other children. As he gradually became less dependent on her, he seemed to withdraw from everything around him. Ruth was struck by the transformation of her blond boy—Will was a towhead when he entered the hospital, but his hair began darkening under the bandages—into the scarred creature who returned. She was outraged when she saw that he was hand-shy. *What had happened up there?*

Will's dreams continued for a decade, and, though those dreams—slowly, like clouds after a storm—became fewer and their power lessened, it seemed to Will—especially during that first spring on the farm—that their hold on his nights would never break. That part of the nightmare of his early life did slacken, but for years the ether of those operations reeked in his memory of some dreadful thing or act beyond his understanding.

## SEVEN

On the long Saturdays in Monticello, he read in the library. He felt safe among the dark shelves. Sometimes, he forgot the afternoon movie and drifted there for long sweet hours reading stories and exploring the lives of great men in a small series of books about American Presidents, scientists, and inventors.

Nurse Alma taught him to read in the hospital before his bandages came off. She described the letters of the alphabet to him, traced them in his palm with her fingertip—and they appeared clearly in his mind, scarlet and gold. Then as she read to him, the letters began to form patterns of sound like his mother's singing. Alma's voice seemed darker than his mother's, perhaps because he was blind.

When the bandages came off, he sought out books. At first the pure black and whiteness of the letters shocked him, but within days after returning from the hospital, he was reading his older sisters' books. That was at first a secret activity; he read alone. He began to seek out special places to read. In the library, Will discovered his own heaven. There he recreated Alma's music and the sweet, burning love of letters and patterns he recognized in her reading.

He still thought of Alma, not as often as that first year home from the hospital, but a part of him listened for her voice everywhere he went. The gentle fire of her voice and songs lit the darkness in his blind eye so that when first one bandage then the other came off, he began to search for writing, any writing, as patterns of sound that fell into groups; then his heart saw them at the same time, and he knew that he was in a new world, one clearly meant for him. Reading caused pain in his eyes. It was simply the way things were.

Will not only read, but listened carefully to everyone's words. He was struck by his father's mix of rough utterance in private and ringing elegance in public. His mother's voice soothed him, her lilting mezzo sharing the same qualities of the hands that calmed his fear. She sang a song in French whose lines descended in a pleasing way, and she also moved in a special way as she sang, swaying as she swept up scraps near the sewing machine, her long auburn hair full of sunlight. Will was overcome by joy—he ran to her and threw his arms around her. Her skirt smelled of sun and soap.

*Oh, Mommy. That's so beautiful!*

Ruth looked down at him, beaming with happiness. It's *Carmen*, she said. I sang it in school, when I was training to be a teacher. The *habanera*.

*I want to sing like that!* Will cried out suddenly.

Ruth looked down at him in surprise, and then looked out the window as if she was expecting someone to come calling. *Maybe you will,* she said slowly. Then, as an afterthought, *You should hear my cousin Dick sing. Now Dick Crooks is a singer.*

### EIGHT

In the library he found a long row of huge reddish books whose name he could not sound out for a long time. One of those books had been left open on the table. Each page had two columns of fine print. His right eye ached as he gazed at the tiny letters. Many of the words were mysterious, very long. Yet he could sound them out, sing them silently. And something told him he could unlock their secrets. They lay peacefully on the page and invited him to stay, like the gentle slope of the pond's levee or a grove of pecan trees he discovered at the center of his father's campus. He began to read about Harvard, an old school in a place called New England. He turned the page, then another; and there was a short powerful word that caught his eye, *Hawk*. He read aloud about how the slender winged creature flew on currents of wind. Then he was in love with the word and so many small words, and then larger words, and sentences and paragraphs and pages and chapters and books, books, books. He carried the text over next to the dictionary that weighed as much as he did. He read it kneeling on a chair.

Miss Jones saw him there, clucked to herself at the thick bandage enclosing the boy's right eye, and guessed his age at four. Then she found a smaller Webster's Dictionary and placed it on a table where he could see it clearly. She joked that he was going to *wear a hole in the floor* running to the larger book.

To Will, she was *his* Miss Jones. She was nice and funny. She touched him easily. Sometimes, he went to the library just to see her. She always seemed to have a kind word. Sometimes he read near the back of the librarian's desk to hear her voice, simply to hear the music in her voice. When the pain in his eyes became so intense that he could go no further, neither read nor sit still, he wandered the dark aisles of the library. *My little ghost*, Miss Jones sometimes called him.

### NINE

On the farm, he could also escape. If he made it to the woods, he was free from some of the things he could not control. If things went wrong when he was alone in the woods, no one was to blame; it was an accident—and that was something he could understand. If an axe cut him or he fell from a tree, he remained calm. But at school, among his peers, there were few accidents and a lot of fear. That was more difficult to understand. Will knew he was different and grew to understand that others didn't like it that his eyes were uneven. Though he rarely looked at his reflection, he knew his right eye, the blind one, pulled in. He was cross-eyed.

He never expected the meanness and the odd repulsion his appearance created in others and, to his surprise and misery, in himself as well. His difference, his crossed eye, was caused by accident, but he was treated as if it had not been. He was treated as if he were guilty of something. He was never able to describe what happened in the woods with the children that day, and the other children who were there shrugged their shoulders or lied. *It was his fault*, the older boys said. *Why did he have to tag along?* It didn't seem fair to Will that what happened in an instant three years ago should still hurt so much. A whole year stolen away in the dark hospital. Was he being punished for something he didn't remember?

*He dreamed of it often, the wooded path, with its gray thorns, the blurry pain, being kicked after he was down, crying and rubbing the pierced eye. He woke in his mother's arms as she carried him from the woods to the red brick house on Campus Drive. He couldn't see, and he cried endlessly and rubbed his itching eye until merciful sleep claimed him. When he woke, the pain was still there, and he could see nothing clearly. His father shouted at his mother, and Will understood that what happened in the woods was a very bad thing for them. His father took him to Monticello to the doctor, then to another doctor, Dr. Cook, in Little Rock. That was one hundred miles away, a great distance. Everywhere they went men in white coats shined painfully bright lights into his eyes. His father left him in Little Rock. And the operations began. And then the dreams started.*

On the farm, he came to terms with his own smaller pain as he sensed the pain of the fields and woods he wandered, even in the endless, cold heavens above him, the realms that Hawk patrolled. Pain was all around him. He found dead animals in the woods, all stiff, dry, and eaten away by worms and weather. The bright little eyes that once danced looking for familiar danger were glazed, dull, sometimes simply gone; the little twitching tails were still. Sometimes their skulls and skins were torn open by shotgun pellets, but not from him or his father. Who then? Strangers who passed through?

Atop the tall pine, he swayed for hours in the afternoon and evening breeze and gazed up at the pocked moon, the piercing sparks of the stars; and he howled out his pleasure with the world of wind, cloud, and sound moving about him and enclosing him like a vast, warm blanket of needles.

## TEN

There were bright days, days of hawks hovering over the pine where he clung high up in the swaying breeze. The pine towered perhaps eighty feet up from the center of the acreage. It was where the forces of the fifty acres met: barbed wire fences began and ended in its bulky trunk, the wires grown into the tree's thick skin at different heights. It cornered three fields; two paths crossed at it, one north-south, one east-west.

He ascended the pine's trunk and, skinned bloody by the rough bark and covered with sticky resin, clung to the uppermost mast of the trunk as it bent and swayed in the flooding wind. When the trunk was no bigger than his wrist, he had gone too far and felt the crown begin to buckle. He scampered several branches down and chattered at the storm clouds, leaning out away from the slender trunk. He began to feel the equal strength of his four limbs as he raced up and down his boyhood ladder in a state he would later remember as ecstasy.

He also climbed buildings at the nearby college where his father taught young men to operate the enormous machines whose whirling parts shaped metal and wood; he often climbed on the natural-stone walls of the Fine Arts Building—one, two, three stories up. Sometimes early on spring Saturdays, he ran the mile to the campus, after his chores but just before sunrise. He gathered the pecans that had fallen through the night in the slight grove in the center of campus and hid them in his shirt under a bush. And then he climbed!

He was always drawn to the tower of the Fine Arts Building. He climbed and perched clinging to the vertical plane of rough stones and waited on the sunlight to find him. He sometimes remained still on one spot for a time, like the tiny lizards he admired, trying to integrate himself into the rough, gradually warming stone. Once he went to sleep clinging to the tower about thirty feet above the rose garden. He awoke some time later, still clinging to the shallow ledges of limestone. The sun's rays pierced his eyes, and he felt oddly stiff and cold in the burning light. Slowly, he stretched out the long shadow growing out of him along the wall's surface and, careful to keep his finger and toeholds on the slight ledges, moved up the tower to the roof, where he perched leaning out over the drainpipe with his tongue out, eyes wide and his stiffened, raw hands backed into his chest like claws. He was victorious—the rising sun had found him.

Poised and still, he gazed out over the rolling fields cut through with barbed wire fences until he knew his mother would be worried about his not being at breakfast. Then he scampered—almost like falling—down the warm stone and ran the long mile home down the rutted gravel road in seven minutes. He counted the minutes out carefully by the thousandths, his calloused feet digging into the red earth along the side of the road like dull knives into ready flesh.

### ELEVEN

Will gradually learned to ride horses on the farm, beginning with an old swaybacked nag of the neighbors' but soon thereafter with Lady, the auburn sixteen-hander his father plowed with. He squatted next to the rich rows Lady and his father sliced up from the earth, and, in the dark curling of the red-and-black soil, he felt a part of that reaching down into the earth. He followed the plow, dropping pieces of potato, each with at least one eye, in the furrow at the distance of a long step—one of Dad's, two of his. After much work with the hoe, he poked down peas or beans into the fresh earth or delicately sifted lettuce, okra, radish, or beet seeds into shallow indentures marking the fragrant soil. He studied the quivering of the horse's powerful flanks as she ripped the earth up in heavy waves, and he longed to have that power underneath him, though at first he could not imagine what it would feel like.

His older sisters, Barbara and Judith, and their friends rode socially, sometimes in parades through the streets of downtown Monticello. His first time on Lady was spent clinging joyfully to the waist of his sister Judith as her heels urged the beauty to a trot, then a rough canter. Judith named out the gaits to him proudly: walk, trot, canter, gallop. Later, he sat alone on Lady and took the reins in his left hand, as he had seen his sister do. Once he understood that every sound, no matter how slight, every movement—even his mood—affected the great beast beneath him, he began to find ways to become, as he later thought about it, *a part of the horse*, part of her power and the rhythm of her movement. From the beginning, he felt partners with her.

He was ineffectual at catching or bridling Lady against her wishes. She was far too big and strong for him to handle unless she let him, so he considered their rides together a kind of gift she freely gave him. When he first approached, she chose to bow her high head to the bit. As he slipped the bit in between her lips and the two horseshoes of powerful, yellowed teeth, she almost went down on one knee to allow him to slip the bridle up over her ears. Sometimes he took a sugar cube or a crabapple filched from Mr. Chambers' orchard and sat on a fence post. This was trickery, but it was simpler for him; the ruse did not fool Lady for an instant, and she simply took the sweet and moved away if she was not in the mood to be ridden.

Will rode bareback. The saddle was half as big as he was and far too unwieldy for him to handle. In addition, after he first rode Lady alone, he did not desire the help of others. Once the bridle was in place, he led the beast over to a fence or trough or tree trunk, depending on where he managed to corral her, and hopped onto the broad warm back with its gentle spiny rise in the center. At first, his right hand grasped a handful of the rough mane and his left hand the leather bands of the reins. He stubbornly fixed himself there until he grew to trust the grip of his knees and ankles against the top arc of the heaving ribs. And as she tested him by moving unexpectedly to a trot and back, or sidling to the right or left, he gradually grew accustomed to her dance and let his right hand move in the air beside him or stroke her shoulder or simply dangle as he rode like a prince through the dusty paths and gravel roads of southern Arkansas.

After falling several times the seemingly great distance to the ground, he lost his fear of it and then recognized in the loss of that fear an ability to become far more than he might have been had he never fallen. In the wild tumbling of each fall and the startling, dusty knowledge of the unyielding earth beneath him, he found a kind of sureness in himself. He found that he could recover quickly from having the breath knocked out of him, that if he could move his fingers then his arm, bones were not broken, and that the powerful ringing in his head would fade into a kind of sweet appreciation of the silent echoes that followed. He understood that learning is not always pleasant and often had a distinctly physical dimension. Reading taught him this, earlier.

And he learned about the reward of taking chances alone. Some rare times, Lady and he moved through the evening light almost as one, whether wading into the pond hock-high for a long slurping drink or galloping furiously along a gravel road, spraying passing trucks with gravel. In those moments, he could have been floating on a cloud or suspended high on a Ferris wheel while the operator changed riders below him. And he began to find ecstasy other than in the pine or library to bring him hope and to forget the hospital, where—understanding neither prayer nor death—he had prayed for death, or any escape from pain and being alone.

## TWELVE

The world was full of giants that stalked and thundered about him. The four-legged giants of the farm he felt he knew well. He studied them carefully and moved with ease among them. They were predictable. If he moved too quickly or not quickly enough, they might hurt him—but not as people hurt him. They did not sneak up on him or yell suddenly or whisper slowly or point and call names. They had no words—or no words he understood—though they seemed to speak to each other in some way. Animals wanted to be comfortable, to eat and go along their paths to and from eating and sleeping. They discovered what they wanted from their hunger. They were honest in their needs. The horse did not kick at him without reason or shy without reason. If the cow kicked him as he milked her or knocked over the bucket of milk, it was because he was being too rough with her teats or was doing something else that hurt her.

People were not the same. Even the older kids at school did things much less predictably than any animal. They wanted to appear more important than someone else, or they wanted to win a game or simply to make fun of someone. When he saw people do mean things or cheat, he felt very small and alone. He sometimes felt ashamed as he watched the playground games at recess. He watched boys push others and come to blows over a marble, a name, a word—a single word. His father said sticks and stones hurt, but words didn't. But when Will was called names, he felt a terrible itching in his heart and then a pain in his gut. Sometimes he wanted to strike out, but his mother told him that fighting was wrong; only bad people fought. And not responding led to being called other names, names he sometimes heard in his dreams, names that echoed in his head as he woke up. When his father shook him awake roughly at four a.m., it sometimes interrupted a dream in which he was speaking one of those painful words. His father's rough touch was deliverance.

It was clear to Will that he was an embarrassment to his two older sisters. At school and even at home, he avoided them. Talks between the two girls always seemed to end in argument, with screaming and sometimes striking. Judith always got the worst of it. The horrible things Barbara said to her! It made his head hurt. But little Nici was everyone's favorite. Even Judith and Barbara could agree about that. *My little angel*, Ruth called her. She would often appear near Will, silent until he spoke to her. Sometimes, when he was alone in the schoolyard, Will imagined her near him, watching him.

Sometimes Judith, who was eight, sought him out and insisted that they play a new game of her design. One new game was called John Wayne and Randolph Scott. Judith was always Randolph Scott because she had a black hat. Once, as Will returned home from Mr. Chambers' and climbed the eight front steps to the porch, she burst onto the front porch murmuring, *I am Randolph Scott and you are John Wayne. I wear a black hat and you wear a white hat. I am Randolph...* and then without any warning, she struck him.

He was awakened sometime later by his dog's rough tongue on his face. He remembered the soft crash of something into his jaw. His mouth was full of dirt, and a ringing filled his head. Judith, who immediately ran away in fear of what she had done, later told him that he sailed over the railing on the porch and landed among the half-buried bricks and freshly planted petunias in mother's flower bed below.

Before that he had enjoyed playing cowboy games with Judith, but after that he wanted to design a new game that involved revenge. He designed several but never played them. He was too concerned about Judith's survival in the room she was forced to share with Barbara. And besides, Judith had a mean right hook. Why risk that again? And why didn't she use it on Barbara? Not that he would've.

His mother was too mild and gentle to deal with Barbara, to match her fury, which sometimes bordered on... What? He didn't know. He saw even his father stare at his daughter when she became that way. It was as if he saw not his daughter but a ghost. He knew his father blamed his mother for the way Barbara acted. *It runs in your family*, he hissed one night. *I saw it in your mother,*

*I see it in your sisters, and I see it in your sisters' children.* The boy did not understand then, but he remembered his father's stare and his mother's reluctance to encounter the accusation in his father's words, and he began to understand. There was no solution to Barbara's fury—or not one they knew.

*There is an answer to every problem on earth*, the preacher at his friend Johnny's church said. Will repeated this to his mother one night at bedtime, and she looked at him curiously. Then she made a gesture with her head, a smiling nod-like move to the left as she studied him. She took his face in her slender, rough hands and rocked it on the pillow. *Yes, Will, I believe there is*, she said. Or did she? He was falling far back into peaceful sleep as she slowly and gently rocked his head in her hands. *Alma*, a far away voice murmured to Will. When Will slept well, he often dreamed of his mother or a winged figure resembling her. *Was that Alma?*

His mother and father were very different, yet when they were together in his presence, they seemed more alike than not. His father was brusk and heavy. His voice was metallic and seemed to cut into the boy's ears; he sang the simple hymns terribly off pitch in church and had only a few phrases he sang in a way that pleased the boy. One was *Abdullah, bulbul, bulbul.* That was a short song he sang, for Will alone. Then there were phrases from country songs, one about being on a bayou, with colorful language. *Good-bye, Joe. Me gotta go, mio myo. Son of a gun, we'll have big fun on the Bayou.* He listened carefully to his father's singing. His father sang only two places: when they were alone and in church. His mother sang for everyone, as did his sister Barbara. His father's voice was rough and dark, but his mother's voice was light and sweet. She sang lilting melodies about places far away. *Vilia*, she sang, *O Vilia*. It was a song about a tree—like his pine, but different. Of all the giants, his mother was gentlest and best.

### THIRTEEN

Will went up to his mother as she sang and leaned his head into the small of her back to feel the sound of her voice. He could smell the faint acrid odor of laundry detergent and delighted in the magical quality of warm sunlight on the calico he pressed against the curve of her back. She murmured to him about how good it is to sing. And he clung to her gentle swaying and the joy of hope that all this would be well and that he himself was somehow good in all the mixture of names and violence surrounding them; and if he was good, then this goodness would help him find a safe place in the world. Especially in the morning, he clung to her fragrance and warmth to erase momentarily the frozen terror of his dreams. At night, his nightmares ruled. Knowing that, Will dreaded sleep, fought against its drowning depths. He lay for endless lengths of time in the dark, clinging to the slightest sound from outside his window or within the sleeping house.

Ruth sensed the terrors of his memory after he returned from the operations, and they played bedtime games to help him deal with them. After supper, he huddled in terror in his bed, his legs drawn up away from the fangs and claws of the black panther he expected to strike at any moment. His slight breath barely visible, his heart racing, he sighed with relief when a slight knock on the door sounded, the doorknob turned, and a ray of light struck the wall near his bed.

*Will*, Ruth would call out softly from the bright, warm hallway, *are you asleep?*

*Yes, Momma*, he invariably answered.

*Good*, she whispered and closed the door softly. As she continued down the hallway to her bedroom, he could trace her progress by the deepening squeaks of the rotten floorboards between his room and hers.

Yet, later that same night, he often found her at his bedside when he finally managed to tear himself from the razor claws of his dreams. The pale oval of her drawn face was usually the first thing he saw when he woke. He calmed himself staring into her eyes before getting up to join his father at chores. If it was earlier than four, he apologized for disturbing her and sent her back to her own bed. He cried softly after she left, fearing a return to the vast and violent landscapes of his dreams.

## FOURTEEN

His childhood dreams were of three kinds. The ether dreams that began in the hospital were most horrific; those were the ones that he usually woke from when his father's voice shook him awake before light. He also had violent dreams—later humorous, when he learned to control them—of being chased. And then there were the old dreams, dreams of the yard in his grandparents' house in West Palm Beach.

Within the first six months on the farm, a fourth dream began to appear. That dream was about falling: in those dreams fragile, sometimes winged—yet distinctly human—figures fell over and over, crumbled slowly with arms like great heavy feathers in some vast wind, to the earth. The first of those dreams occurred shortly after he witnessed his mother's first seizure in the hallway. This was December of last year. Ruth was singing and sweeping in the hall, her simple dress golden with tiny white flowers. Then came a soft cry and her heavy fall to the floor.

Slender white dream-figures first appeared during what he came to call his "waking dreams" in the hospital. He was at least partially awake when the figures first appeared in flashes of light. They did not fall then, but hovered above him in a friendly way.

Alone in the black and grey world of his hospital room, Will sometimes gauged his waking hours by the slightest whispers of light that sifted through his bandages. He heard the doctor carefully explain to his father that both eyes had to be covered in the recovery period, even though only one eye was operated on. It was about *complementarity*—this word excited Will when he first heard it spoken by Dr. Cook—*of the eyes*. What affected one eye affected the other. But they did not bind the eyes the same, allowing Will the comforting awareness of some vague light in his dark world. It was the oversights in bandaging his good eye by the doctors and nurses that helped Will keep track of reality. If the thick bandage was askew, precious light leaked in to his left eye—his right eye was thickly packed with Vaseline under the patch, so no light got through—on sunny days when the nurses forgot to close the blinds. Sometimes the aluminum and polished steel utensils flashed dully through the gauze enclosing his good eye.

Most of the nurses did not act as if he were really there but came and went with swishes and clanks. There were the constant cool swabs and stings of shots in his arm or hip. There were, of course, meals, but he rarely felt like eating and all food tasted the same. The nurses scolded him to eat and stayed till he did. He grasped the bowl or plate and spooned the food into his mouth as quickly as possible. Were they watching? Sometimes, he heard them. *Tsk, tsk, tsk*. How he hated that sound. When he finished, he listened for the sound of the door closing. Were they gone?

Alma was the exception. Her voice was different. He met her on a very bad day, the worst ever. Miss Smith, the rough nurse who usually fed him lunch, was there when he awakened from an ether dream. Lost in a world moving from dream to reality, he was terrified and wild with pain. He sat up suddenly as the nurse attempted to place the tray on the bed where he slept. The tray went flying, and Miss Smith found herself covered with mashed potatoes and milk while her patient screamed out at nothing she could see. As Will tore at the bandages on his head, she attempted to restrain him; in his flailing, his tiny hand struck her. *You hit me, boy?* She screamed and slapped Will hard on the face. He fell back unconscious. When he awoke, he was strapped down on the bed, wet with his own urine, and shivering in the darkness. It was Alma who found him later, crying and struggling to get a hand free to claw at his bandages. She immediately released him and took him, smelly and wet, into her arms. He clung to her fiercely, until she put him in a warm bath and washed him, even his hair. As she bathed him, he heard her sing for the first time.

Alma was all gentleness and kindness, full of song and story. She often read to him from books. At other times it seemed she made up stories for him. Even when her voice was tired, she always had time to sit on his bed a moment and say something pleasant. It was after Nurse Alma sang him to sleep with one of her songs that the dream figures first appeared—at first slight, then more nearly complete. He told her about the figures, as he told her everything. *Maybe they're angels*, Alma said, when he described them to her. *Alma*, he said to himself often in the hospital and now, even now. *Alma*, the one he never saw. And so she became the figure of his dreams.

After nearly a year on the farm and over three years since the blinding, those dream figures had become his mother. She fell slow and soft, crumpling ghostly to the surface of what seemed to be thick grass, where she lay pulsing with happiness, smiling up at him as if waking from a long night's rest. When he woke, he found those bright images in the frosty clouds of his breath hovering in the dark canopy of space above his bed.

## FIFTEEN

Once, just before a hard rain, he saw an old tree explode upward near its top. He was immediately deafened by the yellow explosion of lightning, within—it seemed to him—an arm's reach. In recalling the event afterwards, he was certain that the tree had exploded upward, yet he knew from his reading in the library that lightning came *down—descended*, a lovely word—from the clouds. When he described the incident to his father, he only pursed the wide, thin line of his lips and studied the boy quizzically for a moment. Then they went off together to clear brush near the pond.

That day changed the way Will thought of his father. As his father swung the heavy axe, Will cleared the brush into piles. Twice, the axe came near to Will's head. The first time the axe whistled close, Will was surprised by it; but the second time he fell back away from the work, stunned. As he lay and studied his father for some kind of a sign, it seemed to Will that there was a kind of terrible machine-like energy about the way his father hacked away at the dry brush that spring afternoon. A terrible power rose from Ray and circled above the clearing, expanding from the pounding strokes of the axe. Will backed away and went down to the pond to think. It was as if a monster had emerged from his father's shoulders, raging and snapping silently in the air above the clearing. His father did not turn to look or ask him why he was leaving.

He went to the pine and climbed it. A storm came on about nightfall, like a dream. It was a dream he loved because he could control himself in it. He clung to the thin top of the pine and his grip kept him from falling. It seemed to him that everything around him wanted to make him fall down into the darkness below the huge, rippling cone of the pine beneath him, but he felt the wings of Hawk brush him from above, and he rode the tree in the wind like Hawk, now invisible in night's blanket.

## SIXTEEN

He thought about the event in the clearing for several days and steered clear of his father for that time. Then he forgot about it, almost. He shivered when he did remember it—the way he sprang back to avoid the second blow and then backed out of the clearing.

The next Saturday in the town library, the boy read about lightning and storms in the encyclopedia. He read about how a small German man studied lightning, the flow of electric current, by reassembling a large window destroyed by lightning in a storm. The small man found some important secret in the pattern of the broken glass, but the book did not explain what the meaning was. It must have been the flow of lightning. Was it like water down the windshield? There was a photograph of the man lingering over a large frame, his hands exploring the surface of the reassembled glass, searching for traces, for patterns of the awful power that shattered it in an instant. What did he find? Glancing out of the library widow into the shimmering brick buildings and concrete streets of Monticello's city square, the boy saw the pale image of the small man hovering over the surface of the glass, his hands descending to the surface and the surface of the warm glass rising to reveal its secrets to him. Was the secret that another kind of power rose up to meet the power from the sky? Where did they meet? What was the curious pungent smell lightning left behind? The smell of curiosity? Did earth and heaven meet in that instant somewhere above the surface to answer a question in a golden stream of fire?

Hawk knew. And Hawk called out such things in terse phrases that echoed over the pond and dusty fields. Free and far clear, Hawk rode the invisible wind, every feather tensed to create the perfect surface—so different from the dragonfly's ungainly body—and supporting its hollow breast as its lyric form knifed the bright blue sky on the cool breeze far above the pond, calling, calling down to the boy lying on the brambled levee as he studied the water's surface abuzz with walkers and reflections of flying things.

### SEVENTEEN

Headfirst, he slithered down the pond levee through briars and tall dry grass till he was at the water's edge. He turned on his left side and looked out over the buzzing surface of the low pond, his good eye focusing on one tiny skeletal form after another as each hovered above the gray-green surface of the water. There was the dragonfly, cruising with a bobbing motion over the sluggish surface, the movement of its wings stirring the surface into broken patterns of ripples that overlapped as the vague design of the insect's motion appeared and disappeared depending upon the distance of its wings from the surface. The creature sometimes slowed and hung low just over the surface and seemed to reach its head down and feed on the thick greenish-gold fringes that emerged from the depths of the pond. It was a little machine; it sounded like a machine, even hummed and ticked as Will imagined a fine watch would. He feared it, although he knew it was harmless; or was it something other than fear? Why did his breath catch when he came upon them suddenly? At any rate, the dragonfly was not dragon-like; it was the helicopter of the insect world. He saw pictures of helicopters in his father's book. A man named Sikorsky and his father built helicopters together in a state called Ohio.

He glanced up at the sun, which was just clearing the tops of the oak trees to the east. A distant truck spun by, its dusty hum joining the buzzing layer of sound almost visible to the boy lying head down at the water's edge.

Then there were the spinners, as he called the ones who walked on water and moved quickly on their glossy legs—six legs, fewer than the black widow. They were a different *family*, one of the big red books in their library said. (How curious the word for the spider family! *Arachnid*. He said it over and over to himself, as he did all the words he found exciting.) How could they walk on water, like Him in the story of the fishing boat caught in the storm? He studied the surface-walkers. In the bright reflection, he saw the water rise in tiny platforms to each tiny foot that touched it, and, as the light slowly shifted, he saw lines and patterns projecting out onto the surface from each contact the walker made with it.

The surface of the liquid met the air and formed a kind of skin, not just of floating things, but a surface with a tension, with a strength different from that which lay below—as his skin differed from the muscle below or the heavy skin of his favorite milk cow, Sister, concealed the bone and flesh beneath it. (He had seen bone and flesh in the slaughterhouse and in the grocery store, where whole large parts of cows were hacked by hatchets and sliced by curiously slender knives.) Yet the pond's surface was delicate, its lines varied—they seemed to emerge in patterns that bent around anything entering or rising up from the water. He dipped his finger into the water and raised it above the rippling mirror of the pond that rose to reclaim each drop. It was all one liquid thing and so very beautiful.

Other things rose from the earth as if to break free from the awful force that crushed him when he fell from the horse or a tall tree, the force that only Hawk could break. But if Will could not fly, he could climb: the garage, the Fine Arts Building, the pine. Only Hawk moved with freedom far above the earth, calling out to him from the haze below the clouds. Hawk warned the boy of storms. It never failed. Before the thunderclouds appeared, Hawk flew above Will, calling out its sweet, painful cry. *Ahhhh. Ahhhh*, it cried, as Will squinted up into the hazy sun trying to keep the wings in sight.

### EIGHTEEN

Farm life mixed pain and ecstasy. Will associated people—even his own family—with the pain he constantly felt, while nature fascinated him with the variety and violence of its dancing forms. The play of rays and lines glowing on the earth's broad curve at sunset seemed to him a vast vibrating blanket. Whether he lay under an oak and observed the dust rising in the mysterious, silent wind or studied the patterns of the waves formed by the same wind on crops consisting of countless vertical lines—like the stalks of wheat, sorghum, or rice he had seen on farms near the Mississippi as their car passed or the delicate ripples of the young corn he and his father had planted—he was filled with awe at the world enclosing him. That his Hawk hovered, silent and graceful, above this seething mystery was to him a magical sign, a promise that there was something beyond this realm of insistent fear and pain.

He found time to climb trees and buildings and to explore the underside of things such as their house and, when the opportunity developed, the houses of his friends. In nature he sensed a power that determined what he could and could not do—at least within his windblown fifty acres. In that first summer on the farm, he retreated beneath the oak trees or climbed his pine, and once there he closed his eyes and let the sheets of sound envelop him. That was his "day sleep," the time when he embraced darkness in the bright day and let the dying warmth of afternoon reveal its secrets to him.

Then there were unforgettable parabolic creatures that changed his life forever. Underneath the farmhouse, he was concealed in the cool dark world of a dream, a musky dry place with abrupt limitations no matter where he turned. Above him was a dark wooden grid, clouds of boards with the tips of nails emerging like dull stars from the rough brown furrows of the wood, each sharp little spike with a brown coat of rust, nails in all the sizes his father taught him—eight-penny, ten-penny, sixteen-penny. There he could not rise, even to crawl; he wriggled, inching in the warm dust—a strange crayfish from a summer roadside ditch—to get from one slight dip of the dark soil to the next. Warm dust filled his nostrils as he moved.

Above where he lay, in the corners where the joists and floorboards joined, were the spiders, not the colorful garden spiders with yellow and gold markings, but shiny black ones that moved with sudden quickness, their crimson belly sign burning into his eyes like the sun's blackness. He knew to stay away from them; their name was a warning—black widow, a creature of darkness who built her delicate web in the dry corners deep under houses and in woodpiles, far from every creature but him. He lay for hours watching them weave, knowing their power to kill a boy his size, wondering what it would be like to feel their poison moving through his body like fire. He watched the little machines as they went about their work slowly pulling from their guts the delicate strong fibers in patterns, patterns he drew on the dusty earth.

Once he found himself several inches from a widow as he crawled his usual path to the northwest. It had been several days and the web was new. He stopped when he felt the slight sticky pressure and backed off immediately, his eye beginning to focus in the darkness. Against the remainder of the bright sun he glanced before he crawled under the house, he suddenly saw the slender weaver, bright black and so very sharp in form and exact in movement. She moved out of the corner quickly, then paused. Her belly was to him, the crimson hourglass on her abdomen not a foot from him. Then utterly silent and like a little machine she moved slowly down, strand by strand, from the dark corner where its thickest lines were anchored to inspect her webs. Will saw for the first time that there were actually two webs where he previously saw one, one that she slowly swam across with tiny, exact strokes and another she avoided. She crawled slowly, the very silence ticking with each movement of her slender, perfect legs both delicate and somehow threatening, and to within several inches of his face. She was fearless, perhaps blind, filled with knowledge of her own power. He felt an acrid burning in his nose, as if a thousand ants were there. He backed slowly away and lay nearby watching her for a long time. Then he became aware of a pain in his head and realized that he struck a nail when he had backed away from the web. He looked till he found the nail, which was clean of the usual rust on its sharp tip. He knew this was bad, but he was rarely sick and didn't worry.

He went around the new web. He considered getting some matches from the kitchen and burning the spider, but the thought of it made him sick, so he simply changed his usual path. Many things changed suddenly in nature, overnight, and without warning, but most remained the same. The tree limbs held him steady day after day; the wind blew from the same direction most days; and spiders did not attack humans—they sought only to be left alone and weave and lay their eggs and die in peace. Summer was the spiders' time; they were utterly gone in winter and the warm underside of the house was his. He shared the house's underbelly and woodpile with the spiders in summer as he shared the warm rocks of the Fine Arts Building with the lizards who perched alongside him when he scaled and hung from the rough walls of the tower.

He dug in the earth under the house on hot days, seeking the cool red clay that lay beneath several inches of dust and loose clods of brown dirt. There in the clay he hid certain treasures in tobacco cans or cigar boxes. The pale-green wing of a Luna moth was one of his first treasures. He found it in the feed room, glowing in the fragrant dark. He had entered the feed room in hot pursuit of a large rat he chased from the garage. A large smooth stone was cocked back in his hand. As his eye adjusted to the dark, he saw a snake-like tail disappear between two feed sacks. And there on the soft burlap was the moth wing catching the late afternoon light, clear and pale, like the moon in flight seen from his pine perch. He was delighted at its fragile beauty, and it became his first treasure.

Within days of striking the nail, Will became very ill. He shook uncontrollably with fever. Only massive doses of penicillin saved him.

## NINETEEN

The two milk cows were completely different. Will loved one as much as he hated the other. He milked both cows twice a day, seven days a week. He was not indifferent to the experience.

Sister was smaller, docile, with a large udder and teats. She had small horns and didn't mind if Will occasionally hitched a ride to the pond on her back. He rode her into the pond once and she summarily dumped him into the muddy shallows with a quick dip and roll of her back. In her prime, she gave nearly a gallon of milk, morning and night, and generally stood stock still for milking with little movement except for the endlessly swishing stinging strands of her tail. In the pasture, she ate from Will's open hand, never catching his fingers between the steely teeth that could burst a rock-hard kernel or pulverize a whole tough dry ear of corn.

It seemed to Will that she cared for him in her own way. When she came across him sleeping in the fields or among bales of hay near the shed, she nuzzled him with familiarity, licking his sweaty skin for its sweet salt with her rough tongue. The rough muzzle of her moist snout and the licks from her abrupt tongue were a source of laughter and pleasure for Will, quite different from the pleasure of resting his head against her vast belly as his hands pulled rhythmically at her long teats, the air about him pungent with his smell. Sometimes as Will's two-handed rhythm filled the air with motion and the fragrance of warm milk, Sister would turn and try to lick him like a huge dog, her warm breath flooding over him.

In contrast, Pet's rangy, gaunt frame supported a small udder with smaller, shorter nubs of teats that were as often as not scratched by the wire fences she violated with regularity or by the briar patches she waded through. Pet had an ornery strength that allowed her to wriggle like a huge worm through a fence—made even slightly vulnerable by a rotted fence post or a frayed strand of barbed wire—when it separated her from a lush field or garden. She was the cause of more than one endangered relationship with a neighbor and she was single-handedly responsible for most of the fence repairs that Will and his father had to make. When a frustrated and angry Will emerged from the milking shed, referring to Pet as *hamburger*, Ray laughed loudly and said he understood what Will meant, but he could never harm an animal who reminded him so much of his sister. (Will laughed at the time, but in truth he knew his father's respect for Lennie, and Will worshiped her almost as he adored his mother.)

In the milking stall, there was nothing gentle about Pet. She was nervy and shied to the touch. And when her teats were scraped or cut, as they often were, it was worse. The standard remedy for such scratches was a little bacon grease, which stung on application. Since under the best of circumstances, Pet kicked the bucket—and often Will—when her teats were not scratched and since the bacon grease was applied after the milking, those times when Will bent over and found Pet's scratched teats facing him were the source of a very real fear that he might not in fact survive childhood.

It was war and they both knew it. There was also the worst of the worst, those milkings during which yet another unpleasant factor came into play. On those evenings, Pet was not only scratched but had elected, in the course of the afternoon, to lie down in some sort of filth which had to be washed off her udder and teats before the milking could occur. On those dire evenings, Pet had three separate opportunities to have at the boy: when he cleaned her, when he milked her, and when he applied the bacon grease to her cuts.

One late spring evening, Pet kicked Will soundly in the chest as he began to wash the crusted manure off her scratched and swollen teats. Ten minutes later, she put her hoof down into the milk bucket when the boy was nearly finished and stirred the milk daintily until its contents were unspeakable. Will was very angry, but controlled himself until the rangy beast kicked him soundly on the side of the head as he bent to put bacon grease on her teats. Staggering, a loud ringing in his ears, Will lost any sense of control and began to kick and punch Pet's rib cage with all his might. Not to be out-maneuvered, Pet crushed the slender boy, flailing like a windmill in a storm, into the board slats that separated the lean-to into stalls. Already worked up, Will mercifully lost consciousness after struggling for an indeterminate amount of time—for a man standing outside the shed with a watch, perhaps a minute; but for Will a breathless eternity caught in an insidious vise consisting of warm iron ribs in front crushing out his breath and rough lumber behind leaving splinters in his back.

Later, Ray found Will and the crushed milk bucket in the empty stall. Both Will and the hapless bucket were smeared with manure, and Will was soaked with Pet's urine. Her final victorious act seemed to Will the ultimate insult, though Pet's motivation for such an act was probably much less complex. Will's father always referred to this singular encounter as the Gettysburg of Will's relationship to Pet.

Year after year, the pleasure of milking Sister and the relentless dread of encountering Pet ceased only when the cows were infrequently bred and nursed their calves for a time. Except for those brief periods, Will encountered pleasure and pain in the milking shed twice a day, and that was a fully accepted part of his young life, a duty he could not avoid and one that his father believed would make him a man.

### TWENTY

Every spare moment he was not required to work at his chores, Will was off exploring the pond or the woods that bordered on the sharecropper's property to the West. Late spring, just as school let out, was the richest time, even with its sweat, dust, and long labor in the fields—either theirs or the neighbors'.

Among the neighbors were Mr. Chambers and Mr. Burke, for whom he sometimes worked picking cotton or tomatoes. Especially from Mr. Chambers, whose land bordered on theirs, he learned a respect for farmers and their fascination with almanacs, weather and sharing information vital to their survival. Most important among the neighbors was Tyree, a black man who wandered into Will's life to dig a well on the northwest corner of his father's property in spring 1952.

Will was beginning to milk Sister one morning, when he

glanced out the narrow door of the shack and saw a huge figure stride by, a five-gallon bucket in each hand and a shovel strapped across massive shoulders. All this he saw in a dark flash from his milking stool as he crouched beside Sister, her warm stomach storming softly into his right ear. He rushed to the door and watched the enormous shoulders sway away from him, hesitate only slightly to arch over the low barbed wire fence, then disappear down into the draw to the northwest. Every movement of this giant who disappeared into the struggling sun's first rays asserted that he possessed the land he walked on.

Will carefully toted the full bucket of milk to the back porch, where his mother waited. He opened the ragged screen door and handed the bucket in to her. She smiled at the large bucket of fragrant liquid, then at Will.

*Pet didn't kick the bucket this morning?*

Will grinned up at her, the pupil of his right eye pulled far in toward his nose. *She tried, but I was faster!*

Ruth studied him a moment, then smiled the smile he lived for. He simply gloried in it and knew there was one safe place he could go, one person he could trust. *Where's Dad?*

*He's down in the draw with a man who digs wells. Daddy's going to get running water for us.* She smiled in a way that made Will curious. *Won't that be nice?*

Being indifferent to running water and especially to baths, Will had no comment. He moved quickly away from the porch, clearing the yard fence to the north with a leap.

As Ruth turned to her task of straining the milk, she glanced over her shoulder at Will clearing the fence. *That boy can jump*, she thought, and, as she carefully poured the milk into the gauze indenture atop the gallon jug, she hummed an old melody from *Methodo practico: Lasha il lido e il mare infido.*

Will ran toward the small grove of persimmon trees, where he saw his father and the huge black man in ragged overalls. The black man was holding a tiny, forked branch level to the ground as he moved slowly around the persimmon grove's middle in small steps. Will ran up, breathless with excitement. He had seen Tyree once in the woods, their woods, and another time along the road that ran past the Deckleman's place on the north edge of their property. At first he saw Tyree's bulk moving through the bushes and mistook him for a bear, then distinguished human details. As Will studied the figure next to his father, he felt a flash of recognition. This was a grown man who moved like a child.

His father's metallic voice broke Will's thoughts. *Tyree, this is my son.*

The man glanced warmly at Will for the first time. *Yeh, I done guessed it, Mr. Falke. He resemble you some.* He smiled at Will, who smiled back. *What yo name, boy?*

*Will. My name is Will.*

*Will, huh? That is a good name. Strong name.* Ray cleared his throat and Tyree reacted by again raising the witching stick and moving toward Will. *I got a boy yo age, named Josh.*

Will studied Tyree with fascination. *Yeah? Where he at?* Will fell into Tyree's dialect.

Tyree continued under Ray's watchful eye, humming. *Oh, he home, he working at home with his mother.* He went on a while, humming, then stopped dead in the center of the grove. His stick bent slightly downward, then slightly more.

Tyree looked at Ray. *It here. Water here, but it ain't strong.*

Ray glanced at Will, rolling his eyes. *How much, you think, Tyree?*

*I don't know, Mr. Ray. Maybe enough.*

Ray glanced into Tyree's open eyes a moment. *Let's give it a shot, then. See what you can find down there*, said Ray, glancing at the rising sun. *The tools are here.*

*Okay, Boss*, said Tyree.

*And be careful now.* Ray turned to go, signaling Will homeward with a strong sweep of his arm. *I don't have insurance, if anything happens.*

Will saw a shadow pass over Tyree's face as he bent to pick up the shovel. Then Will was stumbling up the hill behind his father's long strides.

*I will, Mr. Ray*, came Tyree's deep voice after them. *I be careful.*

Will glanced back over his shoulder and caught a wink from Tyree before Ray's arm drew him up beside. *The help you get nowadays*, Ray said under his breath.

*What do you mean?* Will asked.

*A witching stick, for God's sake. A god damned divining rod!* His father spoke through clenched teeth, yet with a grim smile.

*Be careful of what?* asked Will. *What could happen?*

His father answered coldly, matter-of-factly. *Cave in, once the well is deep enough.*

Will glanced back at Tyree, saw him carve a shovel full of yellow clay out of the earth. Then he ran to catch up to his father.

## TWENTY-ONE

Ruth was at the sewing machine in the hall, her back warm in the sun. Will sat reading to his little sister Nici, who in turn showed her doll the pictures in the book. The radio played softly as Ruth's foot rhythmically danced on the pedal of the machine. She pushed the layers of material through the needle's stabbing motion, away from her. Ruth listened to the bittersweet song drifting from the radio in the living room.

*Im wunderschönen Monat Mai,*
*Als alle Knospen sprangen,*
*Da ist in meinem Herzen,*
*Die Liebe ausgegangen.*

Its meaning was vague to her, something about May and love. A faint buzzing grew more insistent, filled her head, drowning out the ending of the second verse.

*Im wunderschönen Monat Mai*
*Als alle Vögel sangen,...*

She saw Will watching her.

Will looked up to see his mother very still; she was resting her head in her hands, her eyes on him. She raised her head, caught his eye and winked as only she could. He smiled and returned to the book. Beside Will, Nici raised her doll higher—she was teaching her to fly—as Will read to her.

The song echoed mysteriously. *What could it mean?* Will thought. *It was not happiness.*

As the man's voice ceased and the piano drifted into unbearable sweetness, Will shuddered with pleasure, then saw Nici drop her doll and stare at her mother. Will followed her gaze. Ruth grabbed awkwardly at her head, then stiffened fiercely and drew her body up on the little bench. It was as if she wanted to rise, but could not. Then the sewing machine seemed to spring away from Ruth, as she suddenly rose up shaking to full height, and the bench sprang out from under her. Her head fell back and her mouth opened as if in a high howl, but a loud yawning sound emerged from it. Nici covered her ears, her doll forgotten.

*What is happening?* a voice inside Will called out.

Ruth's body stiffened, the thick yawning entered Will's memory as a cry from hell, and then she fell heavily backwards to the floor. Will had never understood violence until the moment he saw his mother's fall. Her head struck the wooden floor first with a heavy thudding sound that made Will shiver. Then she lay struggling stiffly with some horrid force. Behind her grinding teeth, her heavy moan was held captive.

As in a dream, Will rose and went to her. He knelt at her head, and awed and sickened by the vibrating thing that his mother had become, he took her head and raised it to his lap. Her eyes had rolled up into her head, her skin was gray and pink foam ran from the lips now drawn back dog-like from her clenched teeth.

*Is this my mother?* Will asked himself.

Barbara and Judith stood in the doorway to the kitchen, their faces frozen in dismay. Nici simply stood, staring silently, her thumb in her mouth.

*Get some water*, Will said to his older sisters. They did not seem to hear him, so he set his mother's head gently on the floor and ran to the kitchen where he found a washrag, which he wet from the bucket of cold water Ruth had brought in earlier from the cistern.

When he returned to his mother, she was still. The color of her face was not so gray. The mask was not so strikingly different from his mother's face. And as Will bathed her face, wiping away the foam from her lips and cheeks, he watched her jaw relax little by little and her eyes roll back down. Concerned and curious, he stroked the back of her head and found there a large bump emerging from the gentle curve of the surface.

Barbara managed to call Ray at work, and he was home within half an hour. By then, Ruth was able to sit up, and Ray carried her into the bedroom, slamming the door behind him. Then Will went outside and vomited in the backyard.

Later, when asked what happened, Will told his father as best he could.

## TWENTY-TWO

Will glanced into the rough surface of the hoe he was sharpening with short strokes of the heavy file. He held the hoe's head firmly on the two-by-four back of the sawhorse with his knee. As he bent over the tight motion of his hands, he saw his face, slender and pale, in the hoe's surface: the small, straight nose and sharp chin, framed by the ragged dark blond of his crew cut. His cheeks were smudged with metallic dust from the file. His eyes. He glanced at them, and then studied them. Not as bad as he remembered. He moved them to the right and left, pausing his work a moment. Maybe he could learn to control his right eye, somehow control the positioning of it as he controlled its movement. It might be possible. He considered the blue of his eyes and the way their brightness—his mother's eyes were the same—drew attention to them. Bad luck. He regained the motion of the sharpening and saw that it was becoming keen. As he rhythmically moved the file across the bright edge, up and back, he thought for an instant of the bright sun of the Florida sky, and for a moment he was suspended high in the warm air above Grandpa Crooks, whose outstretched arms waited to catch him as he fell back down. For a moment he was flying far above the earth, crying out in happiness, knowing that he was safe.

He knew something was wrong. He drew his breath and fell back on the soft bed of the backyard's grass, his arms spread wide. The file fell from his right hand and he watched with fascination as a fine crimson line appeared on the heel of his empty hand. He felt a buzzing sting as a thick trickle of dark blood was drawn down from it to the grass below.

Ruth watched her son's gaunt frame as it bent over the head of the hoe, enclosing it so that the hoe's handle emerged stiff and straight from the elastic angularity of his bent frame. The hoe handle emerged from Will's thigh and ran down, driving itself into the thick grass of the lawn. The bright afternoon sun saturated everything—the combination of the boy's abrupt form, how it paused above the four regular legs and the two-by-four spine of the sawhorse, and the hoe handle formed a shape similar to one she saw recently in *Look Magazine*, that of an ancient animal as painted by the Spaniard—the powerful legs of the beast and the softer form of the victim, at once both protected by and terrified of the beast.

Then, she saw Will look up suddenly, make an expansive gesture, and fall back softly onto the grass, as if it were a bed. She saw bright blood stain his upraised hand and run down his pale arm. She moved forward quickly.

Nici squatted under the pale-green umbrella of the fig tree watching her brother sharpening the hoe. She knew he didn't like her following him, so she hid near him, like a *spy*. She said the word aloud and giggled. She watched him work a while, pause, and lie back on the grass. She lay back on the soft warm earth underneath the fig tree, like her big brother. *Okay*, she thought, *I'll lie down and take a nap, too.*

Then Ruth was beside Will, crying out. Nici ran to help as

Ruth picked Will up and carried him to the cistern. She poured cold water over the wound until the bleeding stopped. The cut required eight stitches and Will could not milk the cows for two weeks.

## TWENTY-THREE

It seemed to Will that his father hated everyone. Will learned to never ask Ray what he liked. The list of Ray's complaints was endless. Blacks were no good, Orientals lazy and useless, Jews—whoever they were—were not to be trusted. Most people were lousy or—and this was the worst of all—*shiftless*. Shiftless meant people had no *fortitude*. This was the most important thing to have: fortitude. It was like gumption, only more serious. Will had no fortitude, his father said. He'd never be any good.

*Good for what?* he asked his father.

*Good for nothing*, Ray said, with a grim smile. Will was especially good for nothing now, because he had cut his hand and could not milk the cows for a while. Ray had to do everything.

Worst of all was when Ray said, his voice low and guttural, "God *damn* it, Will!" The first time Will had heard this utterance, he had heard "Goddamn *you*, Will", and he never got it out of his head.

His father never asked Will anything. Every once in a while, Will risked a question as they worked together in the fields or rode a long distance in the silent Pontiac. Ray's response was always terse and exact. Other times, his father would suddenly mutter an unsolicited condemnation of someone or something between clenched teeth or hiss out his disdain loudly in what seemed to Will a sigh distorted by an angry memory. Will sensed that his father did these things whether anyone was there or not, and it made Will feel alone.

On the rare occasions when he visited his father at work in the new Vocational Educational Building, Will was impressed by the ease with which his father moved and conversed with his students among the great machines in the shop. When Ray was a young man, Will knew, one of these machines had, in a terrible instant torn away all his father's fingers—all but one, the right forefinger. Yet his father walked easily now among the gray monsters, his hands in his pockets, unafraid of the massive whirling instruments that once attacked him. Surely his father was very brave.

Will was filled with uneasy wonder at his father's hands, the shiny stubs of his fingers, the way he gripped a pencil between the nubs when he spent hours at the drafting table. At parties, he always found a little girl of four or five, squatted beside her, and played with her hair while telling her how pretty she was. He was careful, as he did that, to exhibit his hands for everyone watching. Sometimes the girls suffered it in silence, but some cried or ran away. Will was deeply embarrassed by that habit of his father's.

## TWENTY-FOUR

Will had no idea a human could be as big as Tyree was, or as black—*purple black* the men who smoked out back at the feed store said—but mostly he was just large in proportion to his surroundings. His broad form was usually swaddled in overalls and the remnants of a cotton shirt. His arms were thick as oak fence posts and scarred with a hundred small ridges and gullies between the shoulder and wrist. His head was fringed with dark gray fuzz and often enclosed by a felt hat. His neck and torso were thick and powerful; his legs, though enclosed by loose-fitting overalls and not given to quick movements, were also powerful like a bear's. All those qualities were made more striking by the manner in which Will met Tyree and really talked to him for the first time.

One morning after first meeting Tyree, Will finished his chores and ran down to the draw. Milking had gone well. Neither Sister nor Pet kicked him, and he took the bucket of foaming milk to the back porch, strained it into two gallon jars and put them immediately into the ice box. Then, although hungry, he turned to run toward the draw and the pile of soil beneath the scraggly persimmon grove there.

The sky was quite clear as Will scampered over the rolling rises of the north pasture. The sun's first rays blinded him as he approached the draw. He raised his hand to shield his eyes and stumbled over a two-by-four. He fell down flat, then scrambled to his knees, and raised his eyes. The ladder ends pointed up from the earth toward the green persimmons. Then an unimaginable figure pulled itself up out of the earth by one huge hand that gripped the highest rung of the ladder.

A drooping hat tilted back from a huge black mask, which broke into a broad smile as soon as the warm brown eyes found the boy. The horse-like shoulders filled Will's view, followed by the enormous torso. From a second hand hung a five-gallon bucket full of clay. With the grace of a boy, Tyree moved from the ladder over the ridge of fresh dirt around the sizable hole—perhaps five feet across—toward Will. Tyree's massive bare foot crushed a strand of barbed wire deep into the soil. Will then found his rough slender paw enclosed in a virtual catcher's mitt of a hand, warm and encircling and crusted with clay slime that smelled pungent and curious.

*Well, there you is. I was wondering when you was going to come down to visit with old Tyree.* The voice was warm as late spring. *And here you is!* As Tyree dropped the bucket of soil, he flipped it over with practiced ease and sat on it. He leaned back and smiled at Will. *Yep, you done finished your chores and now you want to talk to old Tyree. That's good, I reckon.*

And they talked about the yellow, calky soil, the weather, and what Will studied the day before at school. That night, as Will lay in bed, he remembered every word Tyree said, and he wrote them down in his mind over and over, until he slipped into the rare dreamless well of that particular night.

## TWENTY-FIVE

The cinema in downtown Monticello was for Will a kind of waking dream. On the cold wall, images appeared magically as if to belittle and to charge his night dreams. He gradually relaxed back—when no adult sat in front of him—against the wood seat as the shorts came and went, with their fake rocket ships and silly metallic outfits, and he waited for the feature breathlessly. He let the visual wonders and the music that accompanied them wash over him like the icy water at Ozman's Bluff. In the movies, his eye hurt in a different way, but he didn't care. It was another place where he could forget pain in the excitement of the moment. The sound of the orchestra in films wounded him with a rush of joy.

Will first heard an orchestra on the radio. After hearing a Beethoven symphony for the first time, he ran headlong and embraced his mother in ecstasy. She laughed, delighted, and, after she unwound him from her legs and apron, she sat and showed him a photograph in their *World Book Encyclopedia*. It was of a large group of men. She told Will that the man standing in front was the conductor. He wore a fancy suit and held a white stick high in the air. What Will saw as mysterious objects held by the seated men, his mother called instruments. *It's an orchestra*, she said. *What a beautiful word!* thought Will. *The strings are from Italy, the winds from France and the brass from Germany*, Ruth sang out.

Will's dreams had no orchestra, even after that day, and it made him sad. *No orchestra in me*, he thought, *just voices, shapes, and sounds.*

His mother told a story about taking Will to see *Snow White* when it first came to Monticello. They went in the early afternoon. Will had just returned from the operations and everything visual seemed to be a miracle to him. The film started pleasantly enough, then it occurred to Ruth—as the snaggle-toothed visage of the Wicked Witch appeared for the first time on the screen—that Will might be frightened.

*I turned and reached for Will*, she said, *but it was too late. I found only an empty seat. Then, out of the corner of my eye, I saw the theater door bump open way in the back, and a little shadow slipped through it into the afternoon light. I never saw anyone move so fast*, she said.

She fetched him. For the remainder of the movie, every time the witch appeared he grabbed her hand fiercely. She watched him thrill to the film score with fascination.

Sometimes, it was as if he lived enclosed within billowing curtains of light. But the worst times of all were the night dreams, with endless, uncontrolled falling past any sense of control and, after landing, writhing amidst deafening metallic scraping and vast slashing and crushing figures that spread from garish horizon to horizon. His nights were filled with horrid machine-like figures that tore him apart over and over. And then he awoke, screaming and gasping, with either his mother or father or both at his bedside holding him down. And then he was safe in their arms, his eye molten and running fiercely. And he could describe nothing to them, only cling and fight for his breath.

## TWENTY-SIX

Nici ducked under the enormous umbrella of the fig tree in the corner of the back yard and quickly crawled over to where the fence met the feed house. She was careful, even in her state and her hurry, to avoid the piles of chickens that foraged about the feed house then roosted in the fig tree. The musky smell filled her panting nostrils and as she settled behind the barbed wire strands just inside the north edge of the tree, the sweat began to drip from her nose and chin onto the faded rust of her T-shirt. The wire's rusty barbs were close to her blue eyes, but she was canny and avoiding them was second nature. She rested her forehead against one strand between two barbs, the one taut strand of the three that ran from the feed house to the small metal gate with its latch still rattling loosely in its catch since her father dragged Will through it and out to the stump of the massive tree still lying and rotting twenty feet behind the feed house.

She watched her brother fall from her father's grasp and lie whimpering like a puppy. Her father gestured with a jerk of his head, *Get up!* And she heard his strident scream *Now!* And Will did. His father barked again and Will undid the clasps and let his overalls fall. She saw his agonized look back toward the gate, but his father stepped nearer and barked again. Will's gaze slowly lowered to the ground and he bent over and grabbed his ankles. To Nici, he seemed so slender that even bent double, he was barely as thick as her father's thigh.

For the first time, Nici saw her father straighten out of his crouch and rise to his full height above her folded brother. Then she saw the languid movement of the razor strap in her father's right hand as he swished it slowly back and forth. Then he bent over the boy and whispered something that she heard only as a series of hisses, and Will whimpered louder in response.

Then, her father drew back and raised the strap at arm's length, like an axe. As it fell across her brother's lower back, Nici fell against the rough wood of the feed house, her hands covering her ears against the thick smacking sound of the blow and the echoing gasp from her brother. Then, she grasped the wire in front of her.

For Will, the first blow was the worst. After that, it was degrees of white burning until the tunnel enclosed him. With the first blow, the dread was over; the numbing pain he felt possess him with the initial white hot smack brought a kind of relief, beginning its own pounding rhythm and release into the dark that he always awakened from. He would come back; he would not die.

Each blow emptied him of breath and swept through his body like a wave neither hot nor cold but with the intensity of either in extreme. He had discovered that when he looked west on evenings—most "trips to the stump" were in the evening—like this, he could see the red sun falling below the horizon and in its crimson circle he found the black he knew to be coming for him after the seventh or eighth blow. With the seventh blow, he heard only deafening echoes in his head and lost the ability to distinguish the blows or count them. His grip on his ankles loosened, and with the eighth blow he finally pitched forward blind into the bark-strewn soil by the rotting trunk of the tree.

Ruth gripped the gate and watched the man she had followed into Arkansas pound away at her only son. She turned her eyes away and studied the setting sun, its vermilion flood awakening dread in her. Perhaps if her husband offered an apology for what he had done, she could comfort him. She would mend her son as best she could, hoping for the strength to live with the knowledge that once again she found no way to stop it.

Ruth counted the blows: six, seven, eight. It was over. She saw Will pitch forward. To avoid anything that might further complicate the evening, she turned and walked quickly and silently toward the back door. She closed the screen door silently behind her.

Ray stopped at the gate when he saw his wife moving like a shadow through the screen door of the back porch to the kitchen door and his heart leapt in a cold knowing like fury toward her. She saw it all. As his hand touched the cool alloy of the gate he so carefully mounted, his hand shook violently. He dropped the razor strap and placed both his hands on the gate for support. To his amazement, he felt a burning on his back that ran up his spine to his scalp and there tingled with a terrible rubbing. He lost his balance and knelt by the gate until his breath evened. He glanced out to where his son lay in the darkening, red-tainted landscape, then he rose and went toward the porch. Supper would be the worst, but rules were rules: everyone came to supper, no matter what. His father had insisted on no less. Worse had been done to him, and he had come through all right. Will would be fine; he had to learn. Boys had to learn. It was only one day in his life, and boys needed discipline. It wasn't developed in school these days, God knows. Those students at A&M had none, and it was risky working with machines. Will wouldn't become another of those smartasses. He better not.

Will heard a curious melody shaping itself in the darkness enclosing him. *What did it mean?* He opened his eyes and saw Nici sitting next to him, her bright hair glowing in the last of the sun's rays, her solemn eyes studying him. *Okay?* she seemed to ask. He raised his head from a painful twig and nodded slightly. He raised himself further on one elbow and saw that she was now on her feet. Her feet were bare and stained with chicken. Then her hand was on his shoulder and he rolled back on his haunches painfully, then rose unsteadily to his feet.

*Can I ask you something?* She said.
*Okay.*
*What did he whisper to you? You know, before he hit you.*
He looked at her, tears finally beginning. *You watched it?*
*Sorry.*
*It's okay with me. I just try to get through it.*
*Me, too. Eight is pretty much. You're tough.*
*My butt is.*
She giggled, then choked a little. *So what did he say?*
He looked at her a long time. *A secret. A lie.*
She shrugged and put her arm around his waist to begin their walk to the gate.
*He said, this is going to hurt me worse than it is you.*
*Oh,* Nici said.

At the gate they saw the razor strap, its leather strip lying amber aglow in the early evening like a thick snake. Nici spat on it, but Will slowly bent, picked it up, and took it through the gate and toward the house.

Ruth set the table carefully. Judith silently, sullenly helped with the silverware. Barbara was in her room, probably reading. Ray was washing up. It was over for now. They would all gather soon to eat in silence. Ruth saw her two youngest at the gate, arm in arm. She had difficulty breathing as she saw them interlocked and moving slowly toward the house across the yard, the nurse and the invalid. She felt an old lightness flame into her head above her left eye. She gripped the aluminum sink and felt a familiar grinding of her teeth begin. With great effort, she focused to fight the slide; she turned to check on Judith, who was studying her mother as she restlessly moved the forks from the left to the right side of the plates. With supreme effort, the mother smiled trembling at her daughter and forced her suddenly heavy limbs to move toward the stove where the chicken was surely burning.

*What is wrong with me?* she whispered to herself. *Dear God, what's the matter with me?*

## TWENTY-SEVEN

Ray woke at four the next morning, his shoulder a misery. He rose, careful to be as quiet as possible. *How slow I've become*, he thought. *How old*. As he entered the hall and closed the bedroom door, he hesitated in thought. It occurred to him that the razor strap wouldn't be where it should be, hanging from the towel rack on the basin. He had ripped it away last night before he went to drag the cowering Will from the dining room corner. At least Will hadn't run out in the field after he struck Ray. In retrospect, it was clear why he did it. Ray was grabbing and pulling at Judith from his easy chair, and Judith was yelling loudly for help. It was a game, but in the coolness of morning Ray could see that the boy thought it was something else. Still, for a boy to strike his father? No, it wasn't right, not ever.

*Damn it, he dropped it out there in the yard somewhere.* He was at the bathroom door in two big strides, itching to relieve himself.

The bathroom was not pitch dark; the moon's translucent light streamed in on the calm regular surfaces of the small cubicle, imparting to each surface a luminescent quality. There he saw it, its polished leather strap glowing softly above its canvas shadow. It hung where he thought it could not be. He crossed to the window and gazed out over the south fields, and he struggled to swallow something like a cry that rose violently from his past and threatened to turn him inside out.

He saw there in the far shadows the fleeting image of a fair-haired boy running toward the woods. *Faye, is that you?* he thought. A voice echoed far off. His older brother, dead at seven—Dad was never the same after that. And he resented the dark runt that remained. So much loss, so much misfortune. Death surrounded life, enclosing it.

*Stop it! Get to work.*

## TWENTY-EIGHT

Ruth sat high on the sand bank of the Saline River at Ozman's Bluff. Beside her was a picnic basket full of fried chicken and potato salad. She studied the other hearty women on their blankets and glanced down self-consciously at her thin paleness enclosed in an old, loose-fitting turquoise swimsuit. She felt so slow and weak lately.

Down by the river, which was high and swift now, stood Barbara with a girlfriend. Judith was knee-deep in the swiftly flowing river watching Ray swim across the cataract in quick strokes. They were the two athletes in the family. Ray's long arms sliced the dark foaming water's surface, grasping deep at the river's flooding power. A slight thrill at his physical grace ran through her and she looked around for Will. Where was that boy? Probably with Nici. She smiled at the image, despite a chill sweeping up her spine.

Nearby a radio spewed new bebop and Ruth lay back, stiff with expectation. The bright sun felt good on her skin, but she was oddly cold. Her hands began to move against her will. *Something is wrong*, a voice in her began to murmured helplessly. Then, after a moment of awful panic, a peaceful darkness enclosed her like a blanket. Her thoughts were on one level clear. No one had talked to her about her falls, but she knew they must look awful. It was the silence and lack of eye contact. *Seizure*—what an awful word. *First, at Mother's funeral, then in the hall, and again at the sewing machine—waking up with her head in Will's lap—and again now, dear God, no, not now with everyone looking.*

Ruth began to float helplessly and wait for the monstrous rebellion of her body against all control. A feeling of falling began, and she flailed at the helplessness and terror as it seized her. She watched her arms stiffen and rise. She felt her jaw tighten and snap violently. Then her back arched and her eyes gazed sightless into the sun before rolling back into her head.

Will saw the unnatural arc of his mother's back and ran toward her from the top of the ridge. Before he reached her, his father was there, a bright river of water flowing off his shoulders in the sun. Ray scooped his wife up and carried her—convulsing in his arms and gnashing her teeth in some dreadful struggle with herself—up to the car. Barbara and Judith followed, the picnic basket and blanket slumped in their disbelieving arms. Of the ride home, Will could only remember his mother's slight, seemingly gentle convulsions in the front seat, set off against his father's alternating absolute silence and sudden violent cursing.

### TWENTY-NINE

Tyree studied Will as the boy rubbed his eye and wiped away the tears that streamed endlessly from it. *C'mer, Will,* he said, gently. *Come here to old Tyree.* Will stood up and neared him with small faltering steps that seemed to ask permission. *L'me see you.*

Tyree was sitting on the five-gallon bucket. He took the delicate pale face in his huge calloused hands. *No bigger than a sliver*, he thought to himself, *no bigger than a crescent moon, a new born calf. My, my. But strong somehow, stronger than anyone know.* He studied Will's injured eye and saw how it pulled in toward the strong, small nose flaring in pain and alarm. The iris was tiny.

*So you can't see nothing out of it?*

Will relaxed a little, his face enclosed in Tyree's warm hands. *Bright light*, he said, *like the sun or headlights at night.*

*Bright light?* asked Tyree, wondering.

*In the daylight, yeah.*

*It trying to focus, I see it trying. It don't know it blind. It trying to see.*

Tyree pulled Will close, put him on his knee, his great arms enclosing the boy. The boy was encompassed with a strong mix of sweet sweat, tobacco, sun heat, and wet earth.

*Now you listen to me, Will boy*, said Tyree gravely, slowly. It seemed to Will that the man's voice came out of a deep place within him, like a cave, so dark and rich was it.

*Yes sir*, said Will, unexpectedly for both of them, and Tyree studied him closely.

*You listen me, Will boy.* Tyree began again, strangely unsteady. *You lost an eye, I'm sorry bout that. It's sad, but you ain't the only one to lose something like that. My old dad, he work twenty years for Mr. Burke, then one day he pat a machine like it his friend, and when he look down he ain't got no hand there no more—it in the machine. My uncle, he lose fingers in a wheat harvester out in Oklahoma. My mother's father, he die from gangrene when a wagon crush his foot. They all hurt, but they go on as long as they can. I ain't saying that makes yo eye hurt any less. Life done give you a hard time, but you got to go with it. Old Tyree, he lucky. He ain't never been hurt serious.* Tyree leaned back against the slender trunk of a persimmon tree. *I don't know how God choose who gonna be hurt and who ain't, but you done been chosen. You understand me, don't you, Will? You got to be strong. And you ain't alone.*

Will sighed and rested his head on Tyree's massive shoulder. Tyree's hand enclosed Will's shoulder like the corner of a frail trellis.

*Kids give you a hard time, right? Bout your eye?* Tyree asked, his voice measured and thick, a slight growl in it.

*Sometimes. Some do and some don't. Some never seem to notice it, like my family.* Will hesitated a moment. *Maybe they just used to it. Some kids notice it and pretend they don't.* Will's voice tumbled out like seed from a broken sack. *Others never think of anything else.* He closed his eyes. *I don't understand any of them. Mostly I want to be by myself, but they won't leave me alone.*

*It's important to be alone sometimes,* said Tyree, nodding his head, *but you can't live alone. Being alone sometimes can be good. Like when you climb up in that big old pine tree between yo house and mine.*

*You saw me up there?* asked Will, suddenly.

*Yeah, I saw you up there in that wind,* said Tyree, laughing and shaking his head. *I thought you gonna blow away.*

*No, I hang on pretty good.*

*Yes, you do. You hang right on there. You ride that old wind.*

Tyree relaxed, and felt Will relax against him. *Them mean kids,* Tyree began, *them mean kids...* then his voice trailed off. He sighed, *That's how they made, I guess. They always there, no matter where you go. I done thought bout this my whole life and I don't know why people that way. A man have good eyes, a man have one eye; a man white, a man black. It seem to me a man a man whether he have one or two eyes.* He put a rough thumb under Will's chin and raised the thin crescent of Will's face till their eyes met. *It seem to old Tyree that you a good boy, Will Honey. And I think you see old Tyree good, too. I know words hurt sometimes and people try to keep you down, but you be strong. I know you strong. Remember yo family and other folk who are good and you remember old Tyree. Next time a bully pick on you, you tell them to come down and talk to old Tyree.*

Will chuckled a little light laugh like silvery moonlight and nodded. *I'll do that, Tyree, I'll do that. You bet I will.* But he knew he could never involve Tyree in his struggle like that. He knew Tyree was sincere, but it wasn't the boys or girls who would visit Tyree; it was their fathers and uncles. And it wouldn't be when Tyree was digging on his father's land; it would be at night, at his home. There would be guns, gasoline, maybe a cross.

*Yep, I'll tell them all right,* repeated Will, grinning.

*You do that, Mr. Will!* Said Tyree. He rose, placing Will firmly on the ground before him. The difference in their size seemed to Will a small thing.

Will heard his mother's voice in the distance. *Will, chores!* Her voice was light and musical in the warm afternoon wind from the southwest, like the wind chimes in Aunt Lennie's kitchen in Hopkinsville. He turned and saw Ruth next to the barbed wire fence that ran across the top of the slight rise next to the house. Her apron moved gently in the wind, billowing out from her slender form.

*Gotta go,* he said to Tyree.

*You go on and do yo chores,* said Tyree, *but you come on down here again and we'll talk some more.*

*I will,* said the boy, already starting to run up the rise.

*Will,* called Tyree after the boy and motioned for him to come back close again. Will did.

*Will,* said Tyree. *You seen yo father's hands, ain't you, Will?*

*Yes,* said Will, slowly, a puzzled look on his face.

*You remember what I said bout folks losing things, don't you?*

*I do,* said the boy and his face was suddenly full of afternoon sun. And he was quickly in Tyree's arms an instant, and then he vanished into the late afternoon haze separating the lower pasture from the house.

*You be a good boy,* whispered Tyree softly. And he turned to work into twilight to make up for the time given to Will. *That boy climbing everything to get higher and I'm digging down deep in the old earth. Lord, lord. It all good.*

## THIRTY

Will's fascination with insects grew. Their buzzing dance caught his eye and eased the pain in the other. Their tiny, machine-like movements were like the hands of a clock, but the gestures came in bunches, like giants expressing happiness or pleasure. The exactness of their motions filled his dreams; he dreamed of them as machines, not needing electricity but tiny mechanisms, shiny and clicking, their legs dancing like the arms of a pocket watch, their wings moving like a hay baler, their mouths whirling like the lathes in his father's shop at the college. Each of their movements was exact and full of need. Crawling or flying, the tiny creatures drew him. Some, like the mantis, the spider, and the large flies, filled him with a cold feeling like fear.

The flies fed on the large animals he milked or rode. He first noticed the large black flies that gathered around almost anything spilled or spoiled and on the steaming piles the cows or horses left behind. The shiny beads of their furry bodies moved clumsily about the steaming mass before settling, squatting down to feed.

The deerfly and the horsefly were in another category altogether. They were Will's sworn enemies because of what they did to the large animals. The boy pitied the cows especially in their constant struggle during the summer to survive the clouds of insects buzzing around their necks and flanks.

The deerfly was most warlike and quickest, settling and biting where it was least vulnerable, around the neck and front legs. The strong tail could not reach them there, and the twitching muscle masses could not dislodge them. The boy rarely killed one, even though he watched carefully for them. They seemed not only quick but intelligent. They appeared on the opposite side of the horse or cow, and it was only with the jerk of the animal's neck inward that Will would know that they were there, doing their damage where he could not see them.

But the horseflies were insidious. After watching them at work for some time, Will looked them up in the large dictionary at the library: *large, dipterian, with blood-sucking females.* The blood-sucking was understandable—the insect world lived through sucking or devouring. He first studied the piercing and sucking with spiders. Mosquitoes had also made an impression in West Palm Beach, at Grandpa Crooks'. Even in Florida and Georgia, their acrid odor and the pinpoint pain of their bites were fixed in his memory. But it was the flies that continued to fascinate him because they were so clever and caused such misery to those around them. He studied them continuously, each step of their short summer life. And he grew to hate them. It was because of the wolves. That's what Will called them.

Often on the cows' backs, along their spines, he would see small bumps appear in the late spring. Those bumps grew into large welts under the thick hide of the animal. The welts were painful to the giant beast, which swatted them over and over when no fly was on them and occasionally even tried to bite at them, though they were inevitably out of reach along the ridge of the spine. One July, while sitting on a fence and studying the horseflies buzzing around Sister, he noticed a tiny opening in a large welt on her back and something moving within the hole. He looked closer and saw with a mixture of fascination and repulsion the tip of what appeared to be a blunt gray worm. He squeezed the mound of flesh gently and the gray thing wriggled and extended out of the hole even more. Sister reacted violently and moved away quickly. Obviously, what he was doing hurt her.

He went to the shed and got the needle-nosed pliers and a sugar cube. He returned to the cow, enticed her over to the fence with the sugar and climbed up on her broad back from the fence to study the matter. He tried to grasp the puckered tip of the worm with the pliers, but it withdrew quickly when touched. He then reached down with the pliers into the hole and pulled until a large, grayish-brown wriggling thing popped out from the mound. Sister jumped and jerked away quickly. Will tumbled into the dirt, but kept his grip firm on the pliers. He sat up and studied the fat, inch-long worm whose head was crushed in his pliers. He became nauseous as he watched it wriggle furiously in the sunny air. So this had hatched and burrowed in the cow's flesh for all that time, waiting to emerge as a wet, full-grown horsefly, ready to feed again on its living home. Sister, feeling the change in her back and, it seemed to the boy, associating the boy's action with that change, approached him and sniffed at the larva with her great black nose. She found no interest there and idled away to continue grazing.

After that, he studied with care the flies' patterns, the way they laid their eggs under the skin of the docile animals. First, they attacked in large groups. The group distracted the cow and through their constant onslaught kept her tail and mouth busy, while one female squatted near the spine and bit then flexed herself over the bite, pressing her body as flat as possible against her host's flesh, so that even if she should be struck she would complete her mission there. There was something wonderful and terrible about it. Even thinking about it made Will itch terribly. There were so many extraordinary events involved. For example, how could the fly pierce a hide so thick and tough? How could the larva survive there and grow so large? And could it be that flies, as a group, could actually *plan* such an attack? It seemed to him that they must have.

In August that year, when he began to hunt with a bow and arrow, Will killed a wild hare and found its flesh riddled with the writhing worms. One of the older hunters said that Will was able to kill the poor creature only because it was slowed down by worm sickness. *You probably relieved it of further misery*, the older hunter said. One of the boys vomited after he examined the emaciated body of the rabbit, its flesh alive with wolves. Will learned never to eat rabbits in Autumn.

And so Will learned a truth of the fields and of life. No animal can defend itself in every daylight moment, and in that moment the flies would be there, gnawing open the skin and planting the worm within. The poor rabbit, with its thin skin, was especially vulnerable and had suffered the most.

## THIRTY-ONE

The children were asleep. Ruth would check on Will before she followed Ray to their bedroom. On some nights she went to bed later, sat up a while with her memories and her books. She rose an hour later than they did. It was her alone time. She sat now in the old rocker and ran her hands through her hair, loosening it. As it fell about her shoulders, she slumped forward, a long sigh melting into a stifled sob. She closed her eyes to shut out the image of her son pitching forward into the leaves, while her husband coiled above him like a scaled shadow before the burning sun. No, it was too awful. Yet there it was, clearer than ever when she closed her eyes. She opened them and through the curtain of her hair, she let the dim light play across her face in starry lines and secret glowing webs that were familiar and reminiscent of some earlier time, a simpler time. Her strong heartbeat made the patterns of light tremble. She would not cry; that was too risky now; she had to keep control. She breathed in deeply and combed her hair back from her broad forehead with unsteady hands. Her fingers found a bobby pin, and she trapped the left strands of her hair in its narrow pinch. Then she tucked the right strands behind her ear. She stroked her left temple in a circular fashion, her right hand floating down to her lap. She felt a shadowy need to act, to address wrongs she could not define clearly. She saw a victim, she saw a monster; but no solution. They were both her own. She had no answers but to love them both.

She tried to get up, but fell back weakly. There it was again, the first sign of the coming loss of control, the floating sensation before she fell into that haze she awakened from feeling so dreadfully weak and out of place. The look on their faces when she woke was more than fright or pity—it was disgust. She would not let it happen now, though she was alone. She might wake the others. And they would see her fallen; they would see the beast in control of her. How else could she describe it, the lostness she created when it took her? A monstrous thing.

Her hand flailed to the right in panic, and she grasped the smooth bulk of a book. She glanced down at the photograph album and dragged it into her lap. It fell open and she concentrated fiercely on the image, fighting the sliding within her. There they were, gathered around her by the flagpole in 1935, her sixth grade class in West Palm Beach: three boys, five girls. Where were they now? The boys she knew, because she had followed them for the decade after she married Ray and moved north. Johnny, David, and Jimmy—all had fallen in Europe before it was over. The distant nightmare came home in lists and news reports. She sighed and placed a fingertip on each of the three shining pates, then on her own in the photograph. Love. She had loved them, those good frisky boys peeking over her shoulder and into the camera lens. Photos froze time, and we unpack our warm memories from them. The five girls had married, settled, and waited at home on their men. She had passed the war years with her folks; Ray had visited intermittently from his work with Sikorsky in Ohio; and Barbara, Judith, and Will had appeared.

There, she felt better. They had something for those dreadful years. Ray had returned to her; and they had their children. Then, after the war, little Nici came along. Of course, those times were only dreadful as she looked back on them now; then they were simply what was. Now they were in the fifties, God bless them. Things were better. Men could make a living, support a family. Yet Ray was not happier now. To survive the dreadful thirties, the war years, and to be less happy? Was it her fault?

She lifted her eyes and closed them. Thank God, the sinking inside was gone, no uncontrolled slide into darkness. The pages of the book flipped open in her lap, then stopped. She saw the boy's smile in the photograph and covered it quickly with her hands. *Let it be Will*, she thought, *please let it be Will*. Her hands parted. It could have been Will at two—there was the same bright blond hair, the wide-set eyes, broad forehead, easy smile—but it was Buddy, dear Buddy so similar to Will. Her mother seemed ill at ease around Will from the beginning, even to hate him—as much as her father loved him. Why? Because Will was Ruth's and Buddy was gone; and that was Ruth's fault. My fault. She closed her eyes and fell back in the chair. *God*, she prayed, *forgive me. Remember the payment I have made to you for my sin, remember my little Frederick in your arms, and let me rest tonight. Take this burden from me, and I will be your servant for all my days. Amen.*

Before she fell asleep there in the chair, she said with a vague certainty, *I have my Will and that will have to be enough.*

## THIRTY-TWO

Will felt he understood it. It was an important part of his parents' world and was related to machines. The small machines that people carried in their pockets or fastened on their wrists were concerned with it; they measured it, like a surveyor, for their owners. His mother promised to teach him to tell time, she said. *Okay*, he said, *but what do I tell it?* Ruth chuckled and clucked him under his chin.

His father constantly pointed to the circular dial on the wall of the kitchen and raised his voice. Time must be very important. The school bus driver spoke of time. When a student came in later, his teacher said, *Time waits for no man!* So time was important to everyone. And time was generous, as his father said before a meal. *There is time for all things.* All things needed time. *Time for school, Will!* Time was like a measure, a cup or ruler, because there was time for every activity or thing. Above all, there were absolute times for chores both morning and night, and a time to sleep and a time to get up. Meals were the worst times, unless his father was away at a meeting. At meals, Will's father was a machine of time, allowing no waste in stories or fun. Meals were meetings to somberly eat what was there and without complaint. There was time to eat, but there was never enough to eat. Sometimes, Will fell asleep at the supper table.

Will began to see time as a machine, not like the huge machines that hummed and spun in his father's classrooms or the monsters in his dreams, but a vast machine with parts as fine as feathers or dandelions, vague as clouds. It must be cold, he thought, but full of light, sunlight—he thought of the sparkling crust of winter snow on the dry grass. Morning light sparkled with a certain rhythm, like waves of color; noon had a white sameness; afternoon a golden feel to it. The sun drove the machine's power, with its sparkle, its light. Wind, water flowed about the earth, leaving parts of time everywhere—rain, snow. But what started it all, the machine, movement, time? What began it? It moved his hair in a friendly way; it touched him. Perhaps time was good. Perhaps.

He had many questions about time. Did Hawk know time? Did time fly, as his teacher said? One evening, Will perched high in the old pine and watched Hawk circle high above him then disappear into the vermilion eye of the setting sun. The eye began to bleed and slowly spread itself on the horizon, leaving behind a crimson echo. And into this glow the boy spread his arms, and the evening wind enclosed and cooled his throbbing eye. He called out to the wind, sun and time his pleasure in flight from all things solid and hard with pain.

## THIRTY-THREE

Ruth moved from the porch down the steps to the Pontiac in a haze. She had kissed each child good-bye in the living room and struggled to breathe as little blond Nici—her flower-blond hair glistening with Sunday sun—clung to her.

Usually, they would be at church by then. How could she leave them? Lennie would come to help out, as she had for the birth of each child. *Even poor little Fred, God bless him.* Better to go away than to become that monster again. And Ray was sure he had an answer. There were tests to find out. Epilepsy made no sense, though the symptoms were similar. There was pressure on the brain from something unknown, he said. There was a scientific explanation for what happened to her. She would have to return to the white world of hospital pain, but this time she would not return with a child. How would she return? Empty, as she had after her baby's death, after poor little Fred gave up the spirit? *Ah, God, what a horrid void filled her then,* and Ray was far away from West Palm Beach—in Ohio. There was a war and it was his duty. Thank God dear Lennie was there, with her plain speaking and gentle hands.

*All the unknowns, then and now. When will I see these children again?*

Ray closed the passenger door to the car. He turned to the children. *I'll be back before sundown,* he said. Then he was behind the wheel pulling out of the driveway, his mind whirling with schedules and details of the one hundred-mile drive to Little Rock. It was a drive he made infrequently since Will's stay there. Now that was almost paid off, a few hundred more to go. *All that had been for what? For nothing. Was Will better? No. They kept him, tortured him and released him—disfigured. And for that he paid thousands? Damn them, anyway. Dad was right: never pay off a doctor or a lawyer.* He pried his hands from the steering wheel and turned to Ruth, whose pleading eyes, so full of questions, turned to him. *And now this. A tumor spreading like a dark hand over the left side of her brain. Where did such things come from? What if the operation failed? What if Ruth never came home? Was this the last time the children would see their mother?* He dropped one heavy hand and took hers in it.

*No more questions. Drive.* He inserted the key and felt the engine turn over. As he said to Will, as his father said to him, he murmured now to himself, *We'll cross that bridge when we get to it.*

*Another damned bridge.*

Before their home, Will and Nici stood, her hand in his. Will watched the slope of the 1949 black Pontiac move from in front of the house and disappear in a drifting cloud of dust. Barbara and Judith went into the house and still the two stood. Nearby, a fly buzzed loudly.

*Come on*, said Will. *I'll swing you.*

*Oh, goody*, said Nici.

They talked about their mother the remainder of the morning out under the old oak in the near north pasture. The worn edges of the old tire swing marked their legs and arms, but neither cared. They recreated their mother with words and laughter as sunlight flickered across the gentle pendulum of their motion beneath the high tree.

## PART TWO
**Summer/Fall 1952**


Cloudless days rush calmly toward July,
A half way place in my thirtieth year,
To the day we honor men, when old man death
Will be arrested with photographs and fear.
We reach through time's surface for moments
To form a chain, each link fragile as the image
My fingers touch: the wide smile (father omens),
Hands shaped new, Winchester clutched, wide sure eyes.
My photograph and you—comparison halts,
Meaningless, and I must identify
You again, figure out our blind fault
Of the heart, still stalking me when you died.
But my aim is unmistaken; I know
Your heart now, as surely as I hunt my own.

## THIRTY-FOUR

On a warm afternoon in late May 1952, Miss Lennie Falke boarded a Greyhound bus in Pine Bluff for the last leg of her journey from Hopkinsville, Kentucky to Monticello, Arkansas. The bus had left Hoptown at 4:15 a.m. and she was restless to get away from the smell of diesel fuel and stale cigarette smoke. She allowed her long body to relax against the seat, but only slightly. She could not nap. It was an hour, give or take, from Pine Bluff to Monticello, where Ted—she could not say the name Ray when referring to her brother, even though she knew he preferred it—was picking her up at the bus station. She spotted a slur of hand cream on her knuckle and smoothed it in over the large pale freckles that began appearing on her hands the year before. She gazed out the window and saw Johnny run along beside the bus for the length of the cotton field. He was always there, good old Johnny, like the railroad tracks that disappeared into the horizon but were still there somehow. The limits of what we are able to see and God's gift of the imagination to see what is true but not visible! *Praise God*, she murmured aloud.

Her brother Ted was on her mind night and day ever since he bought the farm. Good fortune was not his, not any of the Falkes's. She smiled at the knowledge of the bad luck that dogged her family. Well, you either laughed or cried about it. Ted was a teacher, like their father before he married, and with teaching there was never enough money. She did not resent the money she lent Ted and Ruth to buy the farm. Ted had always traveled around, and saving money was not his strong suit. She knew he would pay it back as fast as he could—every penny at fifty dollars a month. And her money was just sitting in the bank in Cadiz anyway. Family was family.

Lennie liked Ruth right off, though the two of them could not have been raised more different. Ruth was a city girl, and her people had money back a ways. As a girl born in 1914, Ruth had everything or as she was wont to say, *the promise of everything*. Ruth's family on her mother's side was old, *Mayflower* old. But whatever you had in 1929, chances are you lost it. It was hard on children like Ruth, who had come to expect so much. She would have been fifteen in '29. All the stories of loss they must have heard! *Oh, what could've been*. Ruth must have heard it all. In her entire life, Lennie had only what she earned.

Ruth went into her own little world sometimes, but who

among us doesn't have her own ways? Casting stones and all that. It was truly interesting when Ted first brought Ruth to Kentucky, like he was asking permission to marry her. During that first visit, she and Ruth talked about their girlhoods, a little. Their fathers shared a lot in life: neither made a comfortable living for his family, but both were good men who knew more than their share of misfortune. They shared the terrible pain of loss of a first son.

On the third day of the visit, Ruth—with curious openness—confessed her early sin to Lennie. They were walking out near the top of the hill on Quisenberry Lane, flanked by fields of tobacco and alfalfa. Ruth was made to feel somehow responsible for the loss of her younger brother, her only brother. She was babysitting him in the yard when he ran in front of a truck. No matter what Lennie said, Ruth shook and then lowered her head at the memory. She gave terrible details of it, morbid—Lennie hated that and forbade her to repeat them after the first time they slithered from her lips all soft and terrible, like devils of the mind. She needed healing back then, when they first met. And then Ruth lost her own little Fred, her first son. Then Will came, praise God.

Lennie never allowed words to come between them; she cared for Ruth and that was the end of it. She loved Ruth's distant gaze, her quick smile, and her girlish and gentle ways. Ruth was honest and open. Of all the posts, Lennie chose Ruth for the corner of her fence.

The death of Lennie's own brother shaped her life. Seeing Faye, a beautiful blond boy, die so painfully from that spreading infection in his ear haunted her. And she decided then and there to fight the pain of others. She did what she had to do to become a registered nurse. She worked with all healers and learned as much as she could. Mr. Casey was the greatest healer; he could tell what was wrong simply by laying his hands on. She did not believe it at first, but with the weeks, months, and years of work in his office, she witnessed the only thing she ever recognized as genius, a true gift of God.

Lennie was there for all five of Ruth's deliveries—even poor little Fred, who was wizened and whose slight breath wheezed and caught like a heavy smoker's until the third day when he stiffened and stopped breathing altogether. It seemed cruel to Lennie. Ruth's labor was long and intense. Lennie took special pains to be there for that delivery, because Ray was over a thousand miles north working for Sikorsky, near Akron. Thy people *be* my people.

She and Ruth journeyed toward each other through the war years, and since.

Sometimes, life was like the Bible: the plague of the first-born. When Faye died, almost everyone worried about Walter, who doted on the boy. They felt Ted was too young to understand what happened, but Lennie knew that Ted was hurt by Faye's suffering. Two years later Ted's mother, Penecia, died of consumption—just like Elizabeth, Lennie's mother. Great-grandma Sarah Parker carried it from the Trail of Tears. According to family lore, the disease was there in the government trail blankets. Most of those on the wagon train had it; some died early and some lingered on, if they were hardy. But it went into the bones. My God, when the rot got into a family! Was that little Fred's problem, lung rot passed down through the generations? Who knows, now? Andy Jackson could not leave the Cherokees in peace. He drove them out of their homes and killed them on the trail. That old Injun fighter must have truly hated the originals. Why bother with that now? *Let it rest, Len. Nothing to be done for it now.*

But her mind was on it. The Trail of Tears ran through Hopkinsville in 1838, and they camped down by the river for a time. Everyone in the area heard from soldiers that it was going bad for the Cherokees; they were sick and starving, bound for a hard glory. Great-grandpa Parker—the Parkers and the Falkes were long settled over near Cadiz—went down there with a pot of stew, and he shared it with some, among them Sarah Carroway—Karawah, maybe—and her brother David. He fed them and seeing their circumstances said, *I don't think you're going to make it to the West. If you want to come home with me, you're welcome.* They did. Later, David went out to Oklahoma to the reservation, but Sarah stayed and married Great-grandfather Parker, and they raised a family. Their son had two daughters: one was her and Faye's mother; one was Ted's. And that was that: family history. Tough, but there was much hope from that misery; there was little Nici, Penicia's granddaughter.

Just go on to Monticello and see what there's to do while Ruth is in the hospital. Old Traveler Ted would bounce back, stiff-necked as he was. The mean ones always survived—at least those with fortitude. Ted was not the meanest, but he did change from the shy, dark grade school student who loved mathematics more than anything else into a true individual—withdrawn, calculating. But even with the beatings and the dreadful accidents with his hands, he maintained himself. He moved around, what with avoiding home and getting his education and all, and Lennie thought he would never settle down. But he had and it was here, not far from home. Ruth was quite a catch, and Lennie was grateful to her for bringing Ted most of the way home.

Lennie took off her glasses and carefully cleaned them. Her false teeth clicked quietly; they were a trial, but better than the buck teeth she had. Ted still had most of his. He never took Novocaine—tough. Ruth had perfect teeth before the pregnancies, difficulties afterwards.

Ted met Ruth in central Florida when both were teaching grade school. Mutual friends brought them together. That was the late thirties. Times were hard. Ruth showed her a letter Ray wrote her after they'd dated for a time. *Save me a barrel of kisses and a whole lot of loving for Saturday night!* he wrote. That was a revelation to Lennie. Her brother, a poet!

Lennie had no Arkansas connection till now. It was good to travel, a little. They needed her and that was enough; her blood kin needed her.

The bus pulled into Monticello and she saw her brother's Pontiac parked alongside the dusty shoulder near the bus station. Will perched on the hood like a gawky bird. *God bless that boy*—he was grinning and waving like crazy.

## THIRTY-FIVE

Ray stirred, his eyes slitting crusted, then opening slowly to the full darkness of the room. A pitched grey-blackness encompassed him—in it, fading veiled darts, lines, and flexing shapes of his dream figures. He stared at the ceiling as if it were the text of an ancient book, and the barbed fences and heavy oak doors of his dream dissolved to mere gray flux, and then folded softly into the hidden plane of the bedroom ceiling. Alone. The bed was empty beside him. He had slept restlessly since taking Ruth to Little Rock. His dreams were mostly painful; he usually rose quickly and worked hard to forget them. They were of the meanness of the past, his own meanness, and the hardness of this damned life. And there was Will, his crying out in the night. Anyway, the boy had not cried out last night. What could Will be dreaming, to cry out like that? Ray hesitated to rise, again considering his dream of the house, its trim beauty. Just a moment more. Dreams always seemed clearer in the dark.

Ray finished this room, *Ruth's room*, first in the remodeling—hell, it was *rebuilding*—as an act of contrition for bringing her here, to a filthy old place that had been up for sale for a year or more. Ray knew it would have to be torn down and rebuilt from the foundation up, but not the toll it would take on everyone—on his wife, on the children. And so it was that he was discovering, slowly and painfully, the nature of ambition. He did not learn it from his own father, old Walter, who married late and then lost both his young wives to an illness seemingly bred into them. It was different then—you lived with death clinging to you. There was little childhood. Ray knew that better than most.

Ray lowered his eyes from the ceiling to the recognizable shapes of the dresser and Ruth's armoire. The shimmering gray of the mirror above his dresser reflected the window's vista, and he gazed a moment on the slice of landscape he could not yet make out—although he knew it well. *All dark against the blaze of noon.* That phrase sung so many years ago. The famous singer in a bar, railing against "the Met," as he called it. *Who is satisfied with that damned place?* he sneered in his over-resonant baritone. And he was right. Culture, what good was it? Hell, Shakespeare's works were so dirty that the librarian in Bowling Green kept them in a locked room.

*Enough. It was four a.m. and time to get up and at it.* He glanced once more into the mirror's reflection, trying to make out the fences, then the woods beyond the first plowed field. Then he was erect on the edge of the bed. He awakened at four o'clock for most of his youth and he returned to that cycle when he bought these fifty acres. A dream come true. Or a dream gone bad? It was hard to know when so much of what was right seemed to have gone wrong in the last several years. Ruth was gone. But she would come back and help him with Barbara and Will. Judith was fine, steady, the only one of the four who walked like she was going somewhere. And little Nici, she was with Will mostly, not her sisters. Strange, how children trusted and were unafraid. Thank God Lennie had come. She had a way with kids. She raised Ray, in part—the better part.

*Up and at 'em!*

His socked feet hit the fine oak floor boards and his two hundred pounds lumbered quickly into the bathroom to shave, then wake Will. Ray pulled the familiar string on the 60-watt bulb above the basin, and the dark lines of his heavy face appeared in the mirror before him. He reached into the porcelain bowl on the stool beside the basin and dashed two handfuls of icy water into his face. *By God, that'll wake you up!* He grabbed a rough towel and wiped his forehead and eyes, leaving his cheeks and chin wet. His stubble was as his hair now was, black shot through with gray, thick and coarse. The hair on his head had thinned to bareness on the top. *Just like old dad*, he murmured. *We become our fathers sooner or later.* He ran his hand over his balding pate and down his right cheek, then absently slapped the roughness there. He caught his eyes and held them a moment. Blue. Will's the same. Those eyes—ruined.

He wet the shaving brush in the bowl, then swirled it on the fragrant mound of soap at the bottom of the mug. The thin paste welled up and he brushed it onto his face. He gazed into the mirror. *Don't stop to think about her, just start the day. She'll be back soon.* He took his straight razor, lying cool in its delicate cotton bag, from behind the mirror; and he drew it from the bag, enjoying the glimmer of the polished steel as he unfolded the blade from its ivory handle. He automatically reached with his left hand for the razor strap and raised it to the motion of his right hand in its delicate back and forth pattern. And the razor brushed the leather strap rhythmically until he sensed no resistance to the motion. Then he shaved, sighing after each long pulling motion down his cheek, then up and around his chin. *Will has that same chin*, he chuckled, *and it's a hard one to shave!* His mask tensed as he replaced his razor in its cloth bag, splashed cold water on his face again, and dried it with the rough towel. He patted on the aftershave and savored the pleasant sting along the surface of his face. *And so we scrape our dark souls from our faces each day.*

He returned to the bedroom, dressed in his work pants and cotton shirt Ruth fashioned for him from feedsack; then he strode to Will's room. As he neared the door, he heard Will's keening, and in one accustomed movement opened the door and was beside his son on the bed. He shook the boy roughly awake, allowed himself to be hugged wildly, then pulled away and moved quietly down the hall and out the back door toward the fields. This morning he had the small field near the big pine to hoe, weeds everywhere. Will would help him an hour, then take care of the feeding and milking.

He must earn his breakfast.

## THIRTY-SIX

Nici sat atop the shed. The golden-haired girl faced northwest, in the same direction that the rusty tin roof sloped toward the pond. Beneath her, she heard the chickens stir in their roost and the pig sigh as he writhed in the thick mud of his pen. On early summer afternoons, before she and Will began the evening chores, she watched her brother carefully. On days like this, days when he avoided her after school, she grew fretful and followed him until supper. Will's hunger always brought him in, no matter what. Without supper, she thought, Will might stay out there by the pond, never come in at all. She watched his figure walking angrily across the dusty field toward the pond. Sometimes a wild swing of his arm or leg broke his progress; he slowed and paused. His shoulders shuddered.

She knew the older boys on the bus teased Will. Sometimes, it was Jimmy White who lived down the road, across from Mrs. Stubblefield, that one who pretended to be Will's friend. Will told her how Jimmy sat behind him and got him to turn back by tapping his shoulder, first one way then the other, both times trying to poke an index finger into Will's eye. The busload of kids laughed at Jimmy's joke. She felt a cool descending trace on her cheek and wiped at it with her sleeve. She would be glad when school was out. She sometimes saw her brother do things on days like this, things she knew were bad. Now she saw him reach the big ditch before the pond and disappear up to his head into the swimming air at the edge of the ditch.

She scampered down the long slope of the roof, careful with the knowledge that one slip on the rusty tin might mean tetanus shots. Will told her that. She hurried through the potato patch past the salt lick toward the woods west of the pond. There she climbed an oak and, perching, watched her big brother at the levee.

In the ditch Will found a dry stick, the twigs at its end a grasping hand. He raised it up and placed the hand within the golden and black circle of the sun. He stared at it until everything was black and the pain in his eye became a dull ache. He stood firmly on one leg gazing into the sun, blind with pain but removed from the world around him. After a short time, he crumbled lightly to the ground.

His sister passed near him, but did not touch him, on her way to her oak perch. She whistled her tune, softly. It was one mother had sung to her.

He awoke some time later in the dust. The pain in his right eye was not as sharp as before. He moved the twenty yards to the levee in a dream, not sensing the dust on his face or the broken stick in his hand.

He settled in the tall weeds at the pond's edge and leaned out over the water's surface. He stared at the reflection in the surface of the brackish water. He didn't blame them for what they did—still, he hated them. He studied his eyes, the way the dancing unsteady iris of his right eye pulled in toward his nose. *Cross-eyed.* They laughed, but he never cried as they stared and called out those names. That was what they wanted. He stared back at them, and then it all became worse. His stare angered them, and they struck out at him. *Freak!*

Suddenly he struck out at them, smashing the face reflected in the water before him. He fell into the water, flailing, terrible sounds tearing themselves from his mouth. His face broke the surface and lodged momentarily in the warm slime of the shallow pond bottom. In that moment, he felt small things in the mud wriggling across the skin of his face. His hands grasped the pond bottom and filled with mud as they closed. He raised his head up above the surface, pulled himself out onto the levee, and fell back among the weeds and briars.

When he awoke later, the crimson sun was glinting in the yellow grass that arched low over his face. The mud mask was stiff and cold, his eye a mere ache. His mouth tasted of sulfur. Will sat up and cleaned his face at the water's edge. There were marks in the mud where his hands grasped the wet earth in anger. Will did not recognize them at that time but would later recall these personal runes with pleasure. He glanced at the sky through the western trees and rose, heard his father's voice barking out his name in the distance, and, as he ran toward the shed, caught the slightest spark of gold high in a nearby oak.

Nici remained in her perch till Will was well past the sheds.

## THIRTY-SEVEN

Ruth lay in the hospital bed and thought of Will. Since she entered the hospital, she often thought of him. That he had been here, alone, for so long. The awful food, the indifferent nurses—how different from Lennie—and the cold metal everywhere. The smells of ammonia and ether never left her; it seemed she no longer tasted food clearly. She missed her kitchen, even in its farm crudeness. The nurses angered her. Each time she heard an unkind remark, she wanted to look the woman in the eyes and ask, *Are you the one who struck my son?*

When Will lost his eye, they were still living in the old President's house, on College Drive. Her first clear memories of him after his return from the operations in Little Rock were of the endless hours he spent buried in her arms. He was skin and bones. There was a constant violence about his needs at first. He did not ask to be held; he roughly insisted. He ate wildly, never satisfied. He silently sought her out wherever she was and clung to her. She never had enough time for him during the day, what with little Nici, but when he cried out at night, she went and held him until he slept again. Gradually, after a month or so of his clinging and her changing his eye patch once a day, she began to win her son back. She watched him looking out the window, watching the neighborhood children play. Occasionally, he asked her to name each child, especially those who were with him in the woods that day. She knew what happened to his eye—the thorn breaking open the lens—but not why he was so bruised up. None of the children talked about it, and Will would not answer her questions. *What mysteries children are. How did so many survive? Ah, some didn't.*

Mostly, she remembered Will's clinging. She encouraged him to play with other children along College Drive, especially the three older boys, the Masterson boys, down on the corner. They were with him that day in the woods. After all, they were scouts and always spoke very politely to her. But Will would not play with them, or any of the children who were in the woods that day—not even his sisters. Later, during the year or two in the house on Lake Shore Drive, he made new friends. Greg Fate was one, and that little Kay Griner was nice.

During the first year of his recovery, he had a penicillin shot twice a week. The first time they entered the small white college infirmary, he pulled back immediately at the smell and at the sight of the large woman in white. Then he went wild as she prepared the needle. It took much of Ruth's strength to hold him back until the nurse could come to her aid. So strong at four! And there was so little of him. The nurse, a large woman with gray hair, remarked, as she prepared the needle for the wriggling boy, *I can see I'm going to have to be ready in advance from now on. He's a frisky one.* Neither could handle Will alone. *I'm going to have to break him in,* said the nurse.

Every Tuesday and Friday the challenge was to find Will, then to get him to the infirmary. It became a neighborhood joke, and other mothers came to Ruth's aid. Mrs. Masterson was not among them, a fact that did not escape Ruth. More than once, some of the older boys or a college student ran Will down and carried him kicking and screaming, his eye patch often torn asunder, to the infirmary. Ruth alone never laughed at his pathetic, desperate attempts to avoid the figure in white that tore down her son's shorts while the others laughed. And Ruth alone received his gasping clinging embrace when it was all over. Each of Will's defeats was terrible to her in a way she could not describe. She gave him all she could. A little childhood was better than none.

*Only time I've ever broken a needle in my career*, the nurse was fond of saying, *was that Falke boy.*

Ruth's nurse arrived to take her into the operating room. She was slender, blond. *Lovely as an angel*, Ruth thought. *Maybe I'll die now and go to heaven, if there is one.* The slight nurse whispered something pleasant to Ruth after the shot and lingered near her as the drug began to slide her into a far gray place. As Ruth was whizzed by underneath the endless squares of the hallway ceiling, she heard the voice say, *I knew your son, Will.* And with all her heart Ruth fought to grasp the small hand resting on her arm, but it was no longer possible. She turned her eyes up and for a moment saw a sweet, veiled countenance.

*It might as well have been a very old man with great wings, for it was to be utterly lost to her forever. The removal of the tumor, which was extensive, and the adjacent tissue in which its roots were buried took her memory completely and much of her ability to hold or formulate thought in language as well. She lost her ability to express the fragmented images that remained, and among those bits was not the knowledge of Will's hospitalization, or of his vision of an angel who taught him to read in the hospital during the long months that he was blind.*

## THIRTY-EIGHT

As Alma noiselessly wheeled Ruth into the operating room, one hundred miles to the south Will lay back in the bed of thick dusty weeds and listened to the faint buzz of insects. Cirrus streaked the sky endlessly far above him. *Mare's tails*, he whispered, and the wispy clouds, fuzzy blanket of insect noise, and a curious tiredness pulled him into reverie. Who first told him these clouds were called horse clouds? His mother said it first, one day when they were out by the lake near campus. He was almost four. His vision was unclouded then. The day was warm like this one, and they lay on Aunt Lennie's quilt, the one with large stars interlocked, like the forms in his dreams. They sat quietly, and his mother held the sleeping toddler Nici while Will rested his head on her leg. *Look up there, Will*, she said and pointed: *Those are mare's tails.* He nodded his head in dreamy understanding at the horses in the sky, and she ruffled his hair, just as the midmorning breeze had. He closed his eyes now and again felt her hand in his hair.

Will moved uneasily on the rough weeds. Nothing was clear since his father took his mother to Little Rock. His dreams were worse, often now a mix of his own images, overlaid with vague impressions of a woman he knew to be his mother. His fear for his mother approached pain when he remembered his own time in Little Rock, in the yellow hospital building with its cold metallic rails, dull white walls, ammonia pillows, leather straps, and stale sheets.

*He saw Ruth there, alone, her arms strapped down to a bed to stop her from scratching at her bandages. Will huddled unseen somewhere against the high ceiling of a large room and watched the slender figure of his mother move listlessly under starched white sheets, cloud-like. A cry, a wail rose up from her to him, and he started to fall down, tumbling and crying out.*

*As he fell, he began to feel a strange and powerful itching in his nose and grasped a fine line that slowly but with remarkable elasticity pulled him level with a grassy field where he landed softly on the reedy earth. The hospital was lost in the brightness of the late afternoon sun.*

Waking, Will found a long straw in his hand and a furious itch in his nose. There was also a high sound, a stream rippling in the sun. He sat up and looked this way and that. Then the sweet sound was behind him, and he whirled to see a streak of blond hair disappear behind a group of scrub pines.

He smiled and thought, *She started back. If I give her ten count, I'll pass her at the shed and beat her to the house.*

He lay back, humming. *Thousand-one, thousand-two ...*

### THIRTY-NINE

Ruth became aware of brightness all around her. She looked

into it unafraid and when called went forward into a cave of softer light. In this enclosure she felt feathery, as if she were no longer flesh. She was growing lighter; a part of her simply was gone. She thought she could hear a voice.

*There, that's done. Now the roots.*

A slow chill ran through her, and she remembered nothing more of her past life. No Ray, no Will; no pain or love.

When she woke, she recognized nothing. Forms moved around her, rounded forms, but they meant nothing to her. Sounds faded and reappeared. A form with light hair touched her and made pleasant sounds. A man in white came to see her often and spoke calmly to others in the room.

It seemed to Ruth that something important had gone away, but she did not know what that might mean. She wanted only darkness and rest. She sensed dimly that darkness was good. She heard soothing sounds. She felt pleasantly warm. I am lost, she thought. Perhaps this is not a bad thing. And then for the longest time she remembered nothing else.

### FORTY

Will measured his life in terms of singular moments that he felt must be signs of death. Death in animals was a stiffening; a long sigh, and then the breath stopped. He imagined it as going to sleep; dying was like going to sleep except that one never woke up. His Aunt Lennie described it that way to him once. He immediately asked her, *Do the dead dream?* And she looked at him strangely, without answering. He recognized that the violence of the world was related to death. He imagined himself dying as he lost consciousness at the stump or fell from a horse or tree. As the spattering fall back into darkness began, he said to himself, *Maybe you are dying now.* Death, a vast crimson dragonfly, wings ablur.

And each time he woke aching, bruised, and disoriented. Falling from a horse or tree was not unusual, at first. Once he fell from Lady when, at a full gallop, she suddenly shied from a sharp rattle in the ditch along side the clay road. That time he lost consciousness immediately after the gravel road rose up to crush him, but with time that became rare. Falling from horses became something he did not fear. First, he seldom fell. Yes, it was a long way down, but the feeling of flying through the air was wonderful, and he grew expert at catching himself as the ground approached.

Sometimes he awoke dusty in a clay ditch beside the road or under the pine half buried in pine needles. Gradually, he stirred and found he was whole. If he could move each part of his body, beginning always with his hands, he knew he could ride or climb again; and he could avoid the same mistakes next time, and hope that bad luck—the rattle in the grass beside the road, the brittle limb that gave way under a descending leap in the pine—would not appear next time. He learned to avoid the thin, brittle limbs as he leapt from one strut of the pine's tower to the next.

The world was violent, yes, but there was joy: the joy of flight perched on the bare back of a galloping mare, her hooves thundering below on gravel and her long spine contracting and releasing beneath him as his toes clung to the heaving ribs; and the ecstasy of swaying atop the great pine where Hawk's call rang out clearly from the clouds and pierced him, a bright-waking cry in darkness.

So Will's time was marked by such singular events. There were also broader smears of color that were a droning background for cries of pain and whispers of ecstasy, the clinging perch and fall before flight.

### FORTY-ONE

Will knew another kind of flight, or hovering. When did he first fly in that special way? It was wonderful and strange as nothing else was before it. Once when he was swaying in the pine, he looked down on Nici running to the pond and flashed back to the first time he flew like that, far above the earth and utterly outside himself, hovering in the wind. He became Hawk that day on Lake Shore Drive.

It was late in his fourth year. He had returned from the hospital perhaps a month earlier. It was a wind-swept Saturday. The family had moved out of the red brick house on Campus Drive during Will's absence. The new house was at the end of the Drive, away from the lake, beside the dairy farm's pastures and near the trailer park. Will was walking south past the trailer park when he saw old Mr. Barton climbing a long wooden ladder. The ladder leaned on one of the tall black poles supporting the thick strands of wire that ran along the east side of the street. Mr. Barton wore the dark green work clothes and a hat of train conductors. He had a heavy leather belt on and tools of all kinds hung from it. Around his shoulders was a coil of black wire. It all must have been very heavy because as he climbed the ladder, each rung bent beneath his foot. Will saw that each wooden rung was braced by a thick wire that ran underneath it.

When Mr. Barton reached the top rung, he yelled a short, sharp question down to a young man, who Will later learned was Mr. Barton's son. The young man did not appear to understand at first, but then yelled back *Yes* in a high voice. The old man paused a moment, then reached out toward the top of a large gray cylinder.

Then a loud buzzing pop rang in Will's ears, and he watched the old man's form jerk away from the ladder like a fish first pulled out of water. The ladder fell slowly away from the pole as the body jerked violently away from the ladder, which fell slowly and silently to the ground, striking the young man below as it fell. And then Mr. Barton's fluttering body fell like a huge smoking rag away from the gray cylinder to the gravel driveway below, and the horrible buzzing noise stopped.

It was as if all that happened in one violent, frozen moment, the moment before the smell—white, scalding—reached Will. It was then that Will flew for the first time: he rose high until he found himself hovering far up and away from the smell, with only whispering and wind sounds about him. He watched a woman in a cotton dress run from the house nearest to Mr. Barton's blackened form, fall to her knees, and throw up on the grass of her front lawn. The young man struck by the ladder tried to rise but fell back helplessly. Will gazed down the one hundred feet at himself—a pale question mark of a boy—far below, sitting with his back turned to the scene, and he knew that he was the boy that the woman ran to and carried into her house. He knew, from where he hovered high above it all, that he was quite safe. Mr. Barton, however, was not. In the screaming aftermath of Mr. Barton's fall, Will heard the word dead for the first time. He sensed that Mr. Barton had been changed forever, even before he fell; and he learned that this change was called death.

That was his first flight. He was five and the novelty of it never left him. Later, he learned that the Bartons lived about a half mile away, next door to his friend, Wayne, across the street from Drew Central School. Mr. Barton's son was never the same after that. Later that same summer, after he returned from treatment for nervous collapse, the son accidentally killed his mother as he backed the big green Plymouth out of their garage. He was trying to leave the house after an argument with her. She pursued him from the house in tears and stood behind the car in hope—

Wayne's mother, who witnessed the event, assumed—of keeping him home until he took his medication. At any rate, Mr. Barton's son furiously backed the car from the garage and crushed his mother to death. He killed himself some time later in the front room of the house the Bartons had paid off only weeks before Mr. Barton's death. In a single flash of the revolver, the son joined his father and mother.

*And did Mr. Barton dream?* Will wondered. Sometimes, Will felt lost when he thought of the story of the Barton family. He never spoke of the events that day to anyone.

### FORTY-TWO

It was hot and still. The sun's rays pierced the clustered persimmon leaves above where Will and Tyree played chess with Tyree's hand-carved pieces. The clay around the well hole was baked brittle, and Will studied the glimmer of light on its rusty surface. Tyree studied Will's move and pushed back his big floppy hat to scratch his head.

*Sure you want to do that?*

*Yep*, said Will, grinning.

*You sure are something*, Tyree said, staring down at the board.

*It's your move.* Will looked up into the trees at nothing, trying to conceal his excitement.

*Look at this*, muttered Tyree. *I can't believe this!*

*Sorry you taught me to play?* asked Will.

*No*, Tyree's voice comically distended the dark vowel deep in his throat, *but this is the thanks I get?*

*Yep, this is the thanks you get.*

*You! You giving me fits!*

Will could no longer suppress an excited giggle.

Tyree swatted at the boy with his big felt hat. Will ran away, unable to stop his delight in first victory, and then circled back to torment his captive.

*Talk about a sore loser.* Will hovered over the chessboard, while Tyree hunched over it.

*What do you mean?* said Tyree. *I ain't lost this game yet. It ain't over till its over.*

*Whatever you say.*

Tyree slowly made a move. *Yeah, uh huh! You deal with that. Hm-m-m-m. Good move. But!* Will made a decisive move.

Tyree studied the board carefully, pulled down his hat on his broad forehead. *Well, I'll be. Good! But I can...I can...Hm-m-m.* He drew back from the board, looked up at Will and smiled broadly.

A car braked nearby, gravel and dust flying. Tyree rose and jerked around to look in the direction of the noise, which was a good hundred yards away.

*What the matter, Tyree?* Will asked.

*Nothin, Honey. They's jus some men been parkin down there lately sometimes, neath them trees, watchin. They's drinkin, I spec. Nothin fuh us to worry bout.*

Will was worried. When Tyree broke into his different way of speaking, Will always worried. It meant he was not himself. He became what others expected him to be. Of all the things he learned from Tyree, this was maybe the most valuable. Words had a kind of music and that music revealed secrets.

The car slowly pulled away. There was the clank of a thrown bottle. Tyree stared after the car, then turned to find the chessboard upset and the chess pieces scattered across the uneven puzzle of the baked clay. He knelt and began to gather the animal figures he had shaped during long, peaceful hours of whittling.

*It's all right*, Will said, getting on his knees to help, *I know where they were.*

*No. Don't you bother*, Tyree said. *You won, fair and square. I better get back to work.*

Will, choosing his words carefully, spoke through a grin. *You know, Tyree, it's not lunch time yet, but I was wondering if you was hungry now.*

Tyree smiled. *You know I can always eat, Mr. Will.*

*That's good, because you may recall something you said when we first started playing chess. If I ever beat you, you'd....* Will glanced up at Tyree's hat.

Tyree stared at Will in mild outrage. He took off his hat. *Well, I'll be*, he murmured. He studied the hat, then placed it over Will's head, which promptly disappeared into it. Will strutted away, stumbling blindly over everything in sight. Tyree watched him, grinning. *I better get back to work now.*

As Tyree bent over to pick up a bucket, Will suddenly leaped on his back and put the hat back on Tyree's head.

*I just wanted to see if you'd really eat it*, Will cried out.

*Why you little sprout!* yelled out Tyree and started to buck Will around on his back like a horse. Both began laughing and collapsed into a pile. Tyree studied Will a moment, then broke into peals of laughter. He laughed till he cried, and he glanced at Will lovingly.

*You really something, boy, you know that? You really something.*

And he was gone again into the well hole, leaving Will alone on the surface. Will knelt and finding a sharp twig scratched some words for Tyree in the yellow-gray soil. *Fair friend*, he wrote, remembering Tyree's witching stick on the first day they spoke under the persimmon trees.

### FORTY-THREE

Lennie watched them sharp-eyed from the oak trees north of the house, the huge colored man and her slight nephew. They were hunched over a board that ran straight out from the man's knees to where Will's head and shoulders peeked up over its edge. It was noon, hot and still, and the tufted pasture's rolling surface was a quilt snapping slowly out before her practiced hands. She went out to call Will in to lunch, but he ate with the big man as often as not. She guessed Will was colorblind. It was fine; she knew others, good folk, who were. She had seen a lot through the years, from color blindness to the color of hate.

She saw it all come down to Will. Will was Ted's boy, but so like Ruth in so many ways—and he was the spitting image of Mr. Crooks, Ruth's father. Ted took to Mr. Crooks like a second father, a gentle father. Lennie and Ted's father was a very different kind of man. Walter was a bad-luck man, and bad luck seemed too complex to explain—as when bad things happened to good folk. Yet it was natural in some ugly way, like hate.

Lennie hated very little, but she hated to think on her brother Faye. It made her feel so helpless. All the homecare and bed sheets and bloody coughing of her step-mother was not the worst. The worst was Faye's ear infection gone to the bone. He had barely begun school—like Will now. All that pain, that calling out for help, and then the final quiet. There was Faye, Ruth's little brother Buddy, and Little Frederick Ray—all the innocent dead. You just had to trust the Almighty, put your head down in prayer and acceptance, and go on. That's all. But more, you also did what could be done here and now.

Lennie made up her mind early on to become a nurse over at Bowling Green, just as soon as she raised Ted. He was gone at sixteen, a rake and a rambling boy. She never tired of helping others, especially easing the elderly to their reward. It was meant to be: she eased her second mother, even old Walter with his final infection in 1934, the one after his leg caught between the wagon wheel and the loading dock. She asked him to go into Hoptown to the hospital, but he was adamant. *No damned hospitals.* She stroked the thick yellow fluid from his leg, day after day, after it swoll up. Then the leg started dying, and he said he didn't want to live without the leg. *Truth is,* she thought, *he didn't much want to live any more at all.* He wanted to be with his Faye, *his good blond boy, and with his Lizbeth and Nici,* he said. She stayed with him till the end. Then she called Ray from Florida, where he was teaching grade school—had he already met Ruth?—and they buried him down at Dry Fork Cemetery. Walter's age equaled that of his two wives combined. Sometimes the math of life added up. By 1938, Ray was an engineer and a teacher; and he was married to a teacher. Lennie was a nurse. They were able to make their way.

Her thoughts were interrupted when she heard a cry in the distance. She saw Ted's boy jump up suddenly, let out a Cherokee whoop, and run around the persimmon grove that enclosed the work area. The black man stood up, reared back, and roared laughter that washed over Lennie like cool light. She smiled, in spite of herself. Her arm went around the oak, trying to encircle it. Maybe there was a way out of this bad luck. Maybe poor wounded Will was the golden one, the child blessed in pain. He had the need and the love. Maybe his light was hidden under a basket now. He was Faye's age, but so much older in many ways. Had he ever truly been a child? He had gone to her in Hoptown two weeks every summer since the blinding—always serious, exploring things.

She turned back to the house, knowing that her nephew was traveling a path where she could not go, but it was a path she sensed the righteousness of. She would pray that evening, she thought, as she ascended the front steps of the house; she would pray for Faye, Buddy, Frederick Ray, for Will and for the big black man, and the Falkes, and all the other unfortunates in God's world.

## FORTY-FOUR

Will stood near the newspaper rack and let the acrid fragrance of polished cherry wood, pine braces, and newsprint wash over him. His eye buzzed with pain at the bright rays streaming in from the world outside the cool dappled enclosure of the library's vast walls. He hung on the oak rack where the newspapers drifted like his mother's sheets in the afternoon light. The bright panes of the windows opened out onto Main Street and he could see her reflection there in the burning golden surface of the glass.

Miss Jones was at the library desk. She was wearing the flowered skirt that day, the one she was wearing when they first met, when she asked him to hold the ladder for her as she put books up high on the shelves, way back in the stacks. On that day, she brushed heavily against his spare frame as he held the ladder for her. He felt warm but uneasy at the same time.

*How old are you, little man?* Miss Jones asked him softly, almost teasingly, only nicer. She saw him often in the library. She was new to Monticello then, over two years ago.

*I'm six*, he lied, not knowing why.

*Liar, liar, pants on fire*, she sang out softly, poking his belly with a single forefinger. *You're not more than five.* He giggled. *That's better, you little liar*, and she teased and poked him again. *You better not ever lie to me, cause I'll find you out. I know how old you are cause your daddy told me you were born right after the war— 1946, right?*

Will pushed her finger away gently and said, *Maybe*. Her nail was ragged, bitten off.

*Why, you little rascal!* She howled softly, *misleading a lady like that in the big, dark old public library.* Then she hugged him naturally, his narrow frame disappearing into her generous, fragrant figure. *What am I going to do with you?*

He nearly fainted with pleasure and not knowing why, struggled to free himself of her. She let him go abruptly and he fell back on the ladder. She turned and was gone with those long strides.

He called out a name and ran after her. Just before she reached the brightly lit area where the stacks ended, he reached her and threw himself at her, his arms encircling the large, firm hips from behind.

She gasped, *why you sweet crazy little boy. You let go of me right now.* She strained, looked toward the desk. He let her go.

Now, by the newspapers, he could still feel the firmness of her body against him. Now, as he watched, she disappeared into the stacks in long graceful strides, a large reference book on her shoulder, right arm raised, moving easily, her full blouse swaying. He watched her reflection, and she knew it. As with his sisters, he knew what to do—wait. Just being there was the important thing. They would let you know if they needed you.

He shivered. *When would his mother come home?* Her willowy

image flashed through his mind, and he took a newssheet from the rack and spread it on the vast oaken table before him.

On the front page he saw the blurry photograph of a man bending low over a microphone. What he was saying was in print too small for Will to read, but the big print had the name *McCarthy*.

Then Miss Jones's large warm hands suddenly enclosed his shoulders. *What are you doing reading about those awful hearings?* she scolded. *That's a waste of time. Why don't you come help me put up some books now, like a good boy.*

He watched her carefully replace his newspaper in the rack, then followed her toward the main desk, which seemed to him curiously deserted. From the corner of his good left eye, he saw a tassel of golden hair slip through the heavy library door, and he knew they would not be alone in the shadows.

## FORTY-FIVE

The boy grew to understand force and the way things moved in space. They appeared solid, in their place, but they were fighting to stay there. Everything was pulled downward, yet it grew, strained upward. Whatever force pulled him from the limbs of the pine or the back of a horse and crushed him to the earth was defied by flying creatures like small birds and insects close to the earth and larger creatures, like Hawk, who sailed far above the ground. Hawk seemed free of the earth. It mounted and rode the wind as Will rode Lady or the top of the pine in a wind. Hawk dove toward the earth, surrendering for a short time to the force that always wanted it to fall, but it did not. It turned its wings and spread its tail feathers before it hit the earth's surface and settled gently on a scrub pine or fence post. Or it hovered magically, suddenly still astride the invisible fence of the wind.

Will imagined himself Hawk. He ran through the dry fields, his arms spread, crying out in high piercing tones. He perched high on the edge of roofs, and when he could no longer see the wood and tin his toes clung to, he spread his wings and flew. Sometimes he jumped from the roofs, but only those no more than three times his height. He reckoned it carefully. More distance than that caused his knees and ankles to buckle painfully.

And so Will's fascination with falling grew. Falling was everywhere. Fruit fell from Mr. Chambers' persimmon and apricot trees, even as he and Will gathered the pinkish-golden orbs with petal-fine skins from under the trees. Will invented a game: to catch the fruit as it fell naturally from the tree, before it hit the ground. That is how the boy learned patience. Old Mr. Chambers watched him studying the trees as they drank lemonade after a morning's work and chuckled. *It's easier*, Mr. Chambers murmured in his measured, dry fashion, like the dusty soil clinging to his brogans, *to just let 'em fall down and then pick 'em up. A little bruising doesn't hurt; most are going to be canned, stewed, or jellied anyway.*

But the boy enjoyed the challenge of trying to sense the whispered freeing of the fruit from the tree amidst all the other sounds—birdsong, wind song, bee's buzz, grass whisper. He wandered slowly under the trees, listening and watching. And he caught some few, each a perfect fruit, in the white wings of his hands, the long pale fingers delighting in the pungent ecstasy of the small silken globe. Mr. Chambers clapped his hands once and laughed with delight. Will did a little celebratory dance after his first particularly spectacular diving catch, his legs kicking up like a newborn colt's.

Soon after that, on a particular day in the middle of that dry, dry summer, it rained—a really good storm—and Mr. Chambers later took delight in recalling the day of his and Will's famous rain dance. He winked at Will when he described the way Will caught the persimmon waist-high only a half-second after it fell from the tree. Then Will and, yes, he himself danced. When all was said and done, their dance had clearly brought the rain.

And as the rain began to fall that particularly dry July afternoon, Will danced among the persimmon trees with the old man while streams fell as if from a vault. Smashing puddles, they stepped high and mighty through the soaked grassy fields until mud mushroomed up from the grass to the rough surface where the water, moving in rivulets over the dry earth's crust, tried but could not yet wash the signs of their celebration away.

Later, Mr. Chambers solemnly declared in Mr. Burke's presence that he and Will were going to send a bill for their rain dance to the county. Will said it was a fine idea. Mr. Burke, who owned the next farm over, nodded in agreement and said that the letter would be written as soon as Mr. Chambers learned to write. At this point, Mr. Chambers' face wrinkled into the most amazing grimace Will had ever seen. Will wished Tyree had been there for it all.

## FORTY-SIX

Will found falling everywhere, even at the revivals he attended the few weekends he spent with schoolmates. At the small country churches of his friends, people fell in ecstasy with moans and shouts as the preachers chanted and sang out invitations. *Come forward, brothers and sisters, come forward and be cleansed by God's pure light.* And people jumped up and danced where they stood, or they went into the aisles and looked up toward the altar where robed figures motioned to them with open arms. They fell to the floor singing in strange languages and hugging themselves. And they were praised for falling. After a time, friends or family or a neighbor helped the evangelist lift them up to a calmer glory. Then they were led or carried forward to the back of the tent and they talked about the power of what threw them to the floor, made them dance in a frenzy and moan, hugging and singing and sometimes biting themselves and foaming at the mouth. God rolled them about like toys.

At first, Will giggled with embarrassment for them, but quickly he began to study them with wide eyes, full of wonder at the power that seized them. It was gravity, but it was something else, something inside that made them surrender to falling in the way they did. He fell from horses and trees for a reason and he had come to know a certain kind of joy in the falling, so he understood what they were going through, what they were feeling as they fell. It was their flight. He chose to continue to ride and climb after his first fall, and they chose to fall here and to surrender to the falling and even become someone else, someone who spoke a different language and did things strange and wonderful that they could never do in everyday life.

Later, perched high and swaying in his pine castle, he understood that they too were crying out for a vision, seeking their ecstasy in a world of ordinary struggle. The women especially did the dances, cried out their pleasure and moved in ways unacceptable in their normal life's run. When they were called forward, the phantasms of their imaginations, the visions based in the creamy warmth of canned tomatoes and stewed peaches finally broke from them there in the warm benches and open aisles. All of them, mostly good people trapped in routines that wore them down, worked at discovering a new dimension of themselves in reverie and ecstasy enacted as they cried out, fell, and rolled; they foamed and celebrated themselves, sought and found in accepted public spectacle what was denied them behind their rough oaken doors. The spirit moved through them unquestionable, irrefutable, undeniable; it carried with it a wild freedom of the imagination and the terror of true passion, all within the safe haven of revival ecstasy.

## FORTY-SEVEN

Deep in the stacks, Will found a strange book, brown and dusty, about Thomas Jefferson. He opened it and a dry pungent fragrance rose from the pages. Will smiled as a vague memory flitted past him in the dark aisle and settled on the shelf above him, waiting. Inside the front cover page was written in a rusty delicate scrawl the name *Sarah Carraway* and the words *Hopkinsville, October 1840*. Hopkinsville? He would have to tell Aunt Lennie about this! He turned to the title page where heavy ink had stained ornate letters into the thick brown paper. *The blood of learning*, whispered a voice within him, dark and ancient. He began to read very slowly, first the title, *Thomas Jefferson* and the dates of his life, *1743-1826*. Then, just below the dates was a gathering of words in fine print: *Author of the Declaration of Independence, Architect of Monticello, and third President of the United States*. Monticello? He lived in the town of Monticello. There was a building far away that was also called Monticello.

Will went on turning pages and reading, his fingers dancing over the lines, paragraphs, and engravings like pale spiders. He smiled when he read that Thomas Jefferson was a boy who lived in the country like him. He also rode horses. Will hummed and read. The long words he sang out softly and let pass. He read and was beyond pain, encircled by invisible generations and in the pure world his mother promised him. He entered the whirling universe of learning as a Hawk dives toward earth, unconscious of its wings and full with the joy of the thing sensed ahead.

It was in this way that Miss Jones found him, the ancient book in his embrace and its pages wet with his tears. He sighed deeply in the vision she so envied. She stood above him a moment, studying him with a mothering warmth. Then she helped him mark the passage, and together they placed the old book where it was unlikely to be found before he returned the next Saturday. He made her promise to watch over his book. And she did.

## FORTY-EIGHT

The gravel road ran out away from his eye, its darker surface stained with pale brown dust, its two rises rippling in the retreating afternoon light as if the earth were a vast rusty blanket. On either side of the road ran the deep red of clay ditches. *Blood of the earth*, Will said to himself. It was hot, but not so hot as the day before—an August day before school started, a Sunday off before harvesting corn and sorghum, a space of time before evening chores. Fall was not yet a clear scent in the air, yet its presence could be felt in small things like the hint of cooling earth.

Beneath him, Lady stirred her back and flicked a deerfly from her shoulder. She tore off the tops of the tall dry grass at the road's edge and chewed them uncomfortably through the bridle's steel bit. Will studied her bridling motions, imagined himself chewing with a thick wire across his tongue, and grimaced. What had his father said? The Indians rode with a single rawhide rein, or sometimes they just guided the horse with their knees. His father had used only his knees when he was a boy.

When Lady next turned her head to brush away a fly, Will leaned forward, slipped off the heavy bridle and put it over his head, letting the wet bit dangle down beside his left thigh. The reins he lodged between his own teeth, enjoying the pungent taste of the leather. He felt Lady's broad sides through his overalls; he felt every bit of her sixteen hands alive underneath him as she began to move forward down the road toward home. He grasped a coarse handful of her mane. As she moved from a steady walk through a rough trot to a cantor, he concentrated on feeling the rhythms of the great engine of flesh beneath him. His thighs, knees, calves, even feet clung to the billowing sides he straddled. She broke into a slow gallop, her hooves beginning to pound the gravel in a deep rhythm that echoed in his body, and they tore down the road, throwing rocks out behind them like ancient fears.

The red-laced road blurred against the greenish-yellow background they thundered by. As they topped the first rise, Will released Lady's mane, raised his arms and called out sharply over Mrs. Stubblefield's east field, his voice echoing back to him amidst the pounding of his heart now joined with Lady's hooves on the flooding earth beneath them.

At the gently graded left turn where their property began, Will leaned to the left and watched with rapt attention as Lady pulled to the extreme left of the turn without varying her speed one bit.

If a car should round the turn now! He hunkered down and clung to her back and neck. It was a hundred yards to their house on the right. As she floated under him, she began to move across the road, left to right, gradually. As they approached the driveway, Will saw Mr. Chambers' old truck moving up the gentle hill from his place toward theirs. As Lady entered the yard full gallop, the boy glimpsed Mr. Chambers' surprised grimace above the perfect curve of the rough black steering wheel of the '47 Ford. Then he felt Lady suddenly slowing, and he held on for his life. To fall from a full gallop would be too much.

Mr. Chambers carefully parked his old green truck on the road in front of the Falke place, then approached the heaving horse, now beginning to graze in the front yard. The boy hung from her neck like limp canvas. Mr. Chambers first patted the horse's sweaty shoulder, then gently slipped Will, bridle still hung over his head and reins in his teeth, into his old lean arms.

*Wow*, murmured the boy into the sun-scented, green work shirt.

*Yep*, laughed the old man softly. *Yep, that's it*.

## FORTY-NINE

Tyree's well—Will thought of it that way—down in the draw was equidistant from the two country roads that met to the northeast beyond the small group of young trees shading the well. Tyree and Will worked on the well through July into August. On the days that were extremely hot, Tyree emerged from the clay hole around noon, shared his lunch with Will, and proclaimed it "nap time." And, as Will slouched happily near the ever growing pile of cool, slick yellowish clay he and Tyree created, Tyree took six bricks from the pile of yellow brick his father had, in Tyree's words, *bought too quick*. He took three bricks in each hand and laid them down gently. Then he slowly lowered his heavy body so that the back of his massive head rested on the brick pillow. He sighed, *When it this hot, being lazy is just self-defense*.

In mid-August, on a fiercely hot day, after he settled on his brick pillow and let out a long sigh, Tyree said to Will, *Will, I'm gonna tell you what I'm gonna tell yo daddy tonight*. He settled his hand over his eyes. *We hitting water now. I guess you can hear me sloshing around down there.* He raised his head from the brick and glanced over at Will. *But I don't think the water good. It sour. This yellow clay full of something like rust, maybe sulfur. I don't know exactly. Mr. Falke probably gonna want to send it down to the county.*

Tyree yawned big. Will was getting sleepy too. *I don't know what this old draw good for but growing weeds.* Then he was asleep and so was Will.

It was one of the hottest days of August, and humid. Will and Tyree slept almost the entire afternoon.

Will was awakened by a shovel falling near him. He had turned during sleep so that the sun was striking his face. His father's voice!

*Will, it's late. Chores to be done.*

Will was on his feet. Where had the day gone? Tyree was sitting up and rubbing his eyes. Ray crossed over to the well hole and peered down into the darkness.

Will started toward the barn, but waited where he could hear them.

*How deep now?* His father asked.
*Twenty-seven, maybe twenty-eight feet.*
*How far to water?*
*There's some water now.*
*You got some?*
*In the bucket there.* Tyree was quickly on his feet and in one of those remarkably fluid movements that seemed so beautiful to Will, he fetched the large industrial bucket and held it up to Ray like a teacup.

His father gazed into the bucket. Then he took a palm full out and tasted it.

He looked away at the road, then at Tyree. *That's bad.*
*Yes sir, it ain't good.*
*I'll have it tested*, he said. Then, without looking, he raised his voice and pointed it toward where Will stood some fifteen feet away. *Will, run up and ask your Aunt Lennie for a glass jar with a lid.*

Will was off like a jack rabbit.

*And mind you walk back down with that jar*, his father shouted after him.

Work on the well stopped until the results came in. Then Tyree filled the hole and hauled the pile of bricks up to the house. For Will, the day they moved bricks was sad.

For Ray, the defeat in the draw presented him with another problem. He wanted to bring running water to his house. He promised Ruth, and he would find another way, perhaps from the nearby campus.

Will didn't understand the fuss about running water. He hated baths and could do very well without them altogether. When he told this to Tyree as they moved bricks from the draw, Tyree whooped, did a little dance like a great bear, and hugged Will hard for a long time.

FIFTY

During the first week of school, Will led Kay Griner and Joyce Causey back to the corner of Miss Gladden's classroom. They stared where he pointed, at the large moth on the window pane. The pale green wings fluttered slightly, then were very still. They seemed so beautiful to him.

*It's a luna moth*, said Will. *I looked it up. Luna, like the moon.*

*It's b-b-beautiful*, murmured Joyce, her eyes wide and dark.

*And those are eggs, Joyce*, said Kay, pointing, almost touching one of the tiny, mottled beads stuck to the pane of glass near where the moth had settled.

*It's like a butterfly, right?* said Joyce, unsmiling. *The b-b-babies will be worms, then weave a cocoon, then come out with wings. The wings dry and then they fly away. At least, I th-th-think so.*

*Always in threes, her stuttering*, thought Will, like a design. *I think so*, he said aloud, and Kay nodded in agreement. *But we'll see. We'll watch every day and see what happens.*

*Should we tell Miss Gladden?* asked Joyce. *I mean, maybe the others would be interested.*

*No*, said Will. *It's ours, our secret.*

*Why should it be a secret?* asked Kay, sitting down with her arms crossed.

*Because they'll ruin it*, said Will. *I don't know how, but they will.*

The girls looked at each other solemnly.

Kay shrugged. *Okay*, she said. *If you want.*

*Okay*, said Joyce. *You're probably right.*

*Come on*, said Kay. *Recess is almost over, and I want to get a snack at the store. Come on, Will.*

They left Joyce with the moth, to whom she lifted a steady left hand in parting.

*How do you f-f-feel about secrets?* asked Joyce, placing her face near the moth and whispering. The moth shuddered ever so slightly on the chilly September pane as Joyce's warm breath swept over it.

*I know*, she said. *I don't like them, either.*

## FIFTY-ONE

Will didn't want to fight, but there was nowhere to run. No one seemed to care that the fifth grader was calling him names and pushing him back into the corner where the white building of the school store joined the storehouse. He sensed there were lots of kids there, because he heard them yelling. He didn't know how he got backed into that corner, but he knew his shirt was torn, and there was a warm liquid in his nose and mouth. Suddenly, he was on the ground and being kicked. He smelled the odor of lightning and pine resin. In an instant, he saw a shiny Necco Wafer wrapper in the dust before him. He smiled, because it was his favorite kind, the chocolate ones, and he reached out his hand and grasped it. He closed his eyes tight, and waited for it all to stop.

He didn't fight back. His mother's voice was whispering in him, strong and steady. *Fighting is wrong. Bad people do it.* And then he tasted his own blood and felt a sickening shudder run through his body. He looked around him, shielding himself from the kicks. He didn't understand where the teachers were.

Then he saw one of the older boys unfastening his belt. Will could not understand this, and began to watch what was happening to him very carefully, like when a film slowed down before it broke in the Monticello theater on Saturday afternoons. And then there was a stillness, as if he lay a distance from the kids crowded around him, and a calm held him there in a reddish haze of slaps and kicks. And that word he hated so was being called out everywhere around him. Then the boy's belt was striking him, first on his shoulder, then with a sharp, breaking sound on his forehead, near his eye. His vision blurred.

*He was under the pines in the woods near the college again. The children, some in dark blue uniforms, were surrounding him. They were laughing. They pushed and kicked him. Some were happy, but the older ones were seriously angry and yelled things he couldn't understand. Then everything faded into a haze of pain and the voices began to seem far off and muffled. His face was wet and grimy. He was down on the dusty earth and blind and full of hopelessness. There was no running, no help, no escape—just yelling and kicks and echoing laughter. He curled into a ball.*

Will remembered very little after the belt buckle struck him near his good eye, but Judith told him later that the older boy with the belt had struck him again and again. *Then*, Judith said, *you went crazy*. Will did not remember getting up. He felt as if he were floating, and he watched his arms move about him like whirling tools, grabbing and striking whoever they came into contact with. He hurt the boy with the belt bad and hurt several others who were trying to grab hold of him. He heard a high scream long before he realized it was his own voice.

### FIFTY-TWO

That evening Ray had a trip to the stump in mind. When he saw his son, however, he changed his mind. Will's face was swollen almost beyond recognition, his lower lip split open and swollen up like a ripe fig. His good eye was a purplish mass. His feed sack shirt was torn so that every rib showed on one side. He was bruised up and down. Ray had never seen anyone so naked.

*Who was it?* Ray asked.

*I don't know*, the boy mumbled, and Ray saw that one of Will's uneven teeth was missing. *There was a bunch of them.*

*Do I know them?* The father asked, beginning to notice that his son was squinting up directly into his eyes.

*Nope. Farm boys.*

*Mr. Stoddard called. He said it wasn't all your fault.*

*They wouldn't leave me alone.*

*Why not?*

*My eye.*

*Your what?*

*My eye. They like to call me names.*

*Like what?*

*You know.*

*Yes. I guess I do.*

*Well, that's it. They called me names and beat me up. Then I couldn't take it any more and I guess I fought back. I don't remember.*

Ray felt a tightening in his chest and a slight itch in his eyes. *Well*, he said, gruffly. *Go in and wash up.* As his son turned and started into the back door, Ray saw Judith watching him from the kitchen window. She was ten now, sprouting up. My God, they were all growing so fast. *And don't be late for chores*, he called after Will.

Ray watched his boy limp into the house and then pause behind the screen door to look back at his father for a moment. Something in Will's manner made Ray remember shooting a young buck when he was about Will's age. He aimed badly and shot the deer through its mid-section. It buckled, then slouched unsteadily toward the woods from which it had shyly emerged to graze. When it reached the shade of the trees again, it fell and thrashed about until Ray finished it with a single shot to the head. He dreamed about it for weeks afterwards, but did not know it was buried within him until he saw Will studying him from behind the screen.

### FIFTY-THREE

Before his mother returned from the hospital, Will's nightmares began to alternate with dreams of her; he awoke often with her voice in song washing over him. Other times her words whispered in from a sliver of light beside the door. *Will, are you asleep?* But no, she wasn't there. She was away in Little Rock.

He woke one Friday night in October and felt her presence hovering in his room as he emerged from the nightmare—in this particular recurring nightmare, he tumbled endlessly down a long cliff whose jagged edges pierced him, tore his body, while a metallic voice screamed at him. It was a dreadful feeling, to fall so out of control down the spiny ridge of the mountainside. As often in his nightmares, the horizon consisted of mountainous ridges flexing like loose barbed wire in the wind. There was a terrible bright howling in the distance. But now that nightmare landscape and the floating figure that had led him from it disappeared into a soft light flowing from the partially open door to his room.

He sat up, as he became aware that the scream in his dream still echoed in his room as a curious high-pitched whine. It came from the direction of his parents' bedroom. He had never heard anything like it. He knew it was a sound of something not right. It was not like the thick animal sounds that emerged from his mother's lips as she writhed on the floor in a seizure. It was softer, like the cry his dog made as it licked the wound torn out by a big snapping turtle.

Will opened his door opened silently and surveyed the naked joists of the hallway. The next day they would lay the shiny narrow boards in the hall, but that night he stepped carefully from bare joist to joist, and as he did so he brushed against the sack of sixteen-penny nails he and his father used the day before to reinforce the original joists in the hall. He reached the bathroom on his right and continued. Beneath Will was the place he encountered the black widow and cut his head. It was laid bare by their work.

The door to his parent's bedroom was ajar. *Like everything in this damned house*, his father said more than once, bitterly, *nothing fits exactly*. The soft wailing ceased for a moment, and there was silence before the crickets underneath the house began to sing again. *Shoddy workmanship*, Ray said through clinched teeth. And the boy nodded. But it was a very old house, he added, and glancing at the boy he said, *I guess they were doing the best they could under the circumstances*.

The wail began again. Will crept toward the door and knelt down to steady himself. At first, he thought he saw a large boy standing naked at his father's chest of drawers, head in hands. The sound came from that figure which rocked forward and back, forward and back, rubbing his eyes in a vague circular motion as if to press them into his head and then rubbing his face even harder up and down. Then the figure stood motionless, his hands fell to his side, and he gazed forward into the mirror set above the dresser. He whispered a word the boy heard once or twice in Bible school. It was a word from far off and of another time.

*Cursed*, he whispered. *Cursed, cursed*. As his voice died away, he raised his hands slowly to the rim of the dresser. He lowered his head to them and the whining noise began again but it was broken by loud explosions of breath that echoed through the room and hallway like crying, but so unlike his mother's gentle sobs—a terrible kind of heaving Will could not stand to hear. He covered his ears.

A sharp pain hit Will's chest, and he wanted to vomit. He rose, glanced once more at the pale figure slumped against the dresser heaving like a blacksmith's billows, and crawled over the joists back to his room. He fell unconscious on the floor just inside the open door. It was there that his father found him at 4:30.

That day they laid the hallway flooring.

### FIFTY-FOUR

Just before dawn, when early morning light was just beginning to glow on the treetops, Lennie approached the mound where the well hole had been. It was where she saw Will and Tyree playing their game. A recent rain pocked the clay, and the nearby grass was streaked with the reddish-gold of sulfured clay. She studied the area. Hanging from a persimmon tree, she spotted—as if it had been left there to be found—a small, hand-sewn leather bag. The big black man left it for Will probably, but the boy had not been down in the draw since they stopped work those weeks ago. She fetched the bag and found in it thirty-two carefully carved wooden figures: sixteen darks, sixteen light. The dark were stained with chestnut juice; the white were natural and smelled of pine. *Beautiful*, she thought, *too beautiful to be forgotten*. She took the bag and started up to the house. She had a checkerboard, brought from Kentucky. She could learn this game. She knew it was more difficult than checkers, but she could learn it.

## FIFTY-FIVE

Will loved the Monticello library; he loved its red brick walls, rough granite cornerstones, and the thick crabgrass that skirted it. Inside the heavy oak doors, the polished floors required him to wear shoes. (Only Miss Jones knew that, once he was safe within the stacks, he took off his shoes.) To the left of the entry was the main desk and behind it the card catalogues and tall rows of books of all kinds. To the right was the area where he usually worked on his words of the day.

He began the ritual Miss Jones taught him with the dictionary and the encyclopedias. Today it was the word his father said last night, *cursed*. When his father said it, the boy felt something he never felt before; he wanted to laugh, but could only cry. A curse had to be painful. He felt changed somehow by what he saw and heard that night. He was changed, but he could not say how.

Inside him, he carried a second problem, which was on his mind all the time these days. The problem was Tyree, well not Tyree but Tyree's... unhappiness. Well, maybe not that, but it was like fear. What was he afraid of? He found through his Saturday library adventures that not every problem had an answer. Some problems were too complex because they were too old to solve, *like wounds*—one writer said—*too old to heal*. He didn't grasp this at first but memorized it for its music. Then something in him hinted at understanding. His own eye was operated on when he was four. It had not healed. He still had constant pain in it during the day, when the bright sun pierced him like a needle. When he lay down at night, the pain behind his eyelids became a throbbing ache. But when he was reading, the pain went away. In the library, it didn't hurt so much. He moved quickly toward the *Britannicas*.

As he went by the polished bar of the library desk, he heard a low, melodious voice sing out, *Here he comes, my little Saturday scholar.*

He turned to face the blue eyes whose warmth made him feel so at home here. *Hi, Miss Jones*, he said, smiling.

*You beginning at the beginning, like I taught you?* She queried, her voice musical.

*Yes, ma'am*, he said. *Just like you taught me.*

*You are one good boy, Will. I tell you no lies. You are a goodun!* She winked at him, then waved him toward the references with an economical turn of her ivory wrist. *You go on now and do your work. And*, she added, as she turned back to her work, *you tell me what you come up with before you leave.*

*Yes, ma'am.*

*Cursed*, his father said last night before the mirror. Will got the dictionary. It said curses were *divine in origin*. That was strange. In a Sunday sermon he remembered, the preacher said that *people should never curse, never take the Lord's name in vain*. And there was a commandment against it, so that was that. But words were used in different ways by different people. And if a man said a curse, it was different from God's saying one. If God did it, it must be good, but if man did it, it might not be. It seemed to Will that his father was talking to God, as in a prayer. But there was more. Sometimes, when his father or another man was mad, he would say *God damn it*! So they must be asking God to curse something. So his father believed God had power to curse someone. But his father meant something else that night. Will thought that maybe his father meant that he himself, Ray Falke, was cursed. Cursed by who? God?

The boy sat back, his eye hurting him terribly. How could his father be cursed? He leaned back and closed his eyes. He saw his father bending forward again and again, muttering the single word until his forehead struck the chest of drawers softly. *Cursed, cursed*, Ray said, so softly the boy hardly heard it. Now, the words echoed in Will.

So a curse was divine, and this meant his father felt like others who were cursed. The article mentioned two others who were cursed: Job and Oedipus. Job was from the Bible, he knew. He memorized all the books at Sunday school. This he could read in the Bible. But Oedipus? What a strange name. He would ask Miss Jones about him. He wrote down the name on a scrap of paper from the nearby wastebasket. He read more, quickly, skipping the long words that he would have to spend more time on later. There was another word he had learned in Sunday school, *plague*. The plagues were epidemics, illnesses. The worst occurred in the sixth century, during the rule of Justinian. Justinian's hopes for a great empire to give to his sons was ruined by a plague that killed half of his subjects, *perhaps a hundred million people. My God*, thought Will, as he raised his eyes to the midmorning light streaming through the window. He remembered the maps of the United States in the adjacent room where oversized books were kept. There was small print in the lower corner that the population of the United States was two hundred forty million. That would be nearly half of this country. He returned to his reading.

He found a passage that brought Tyree to mind. Some historians thought, the article said, that this plague destroyed slavery in Europe because of *the high demand for labor*. Yet slavery was a part of America, much later. He had read books. One of the first books Miss Jones gave him to read was one that made him sick when he read it, *Uncle Tom's Cabin*. He felt ill and ran to the bathroom to throw up. He was reading a conversation between two slave owners near the beginning of the book. It was the first time it happened just from reading. But he finished reading that book. He had to. If he felt sick at reading about it, how did Tyree feel about it? Was Tyree's grandfather a slave? He could talk to Tyree about it. Tyree mentioned another word when they talked about slavery one day by the well, *lynching*. It was for another day. Today was *Oedipus*.

He went to Miss Jones again, as he had many other times, with a word scribbled on a sheet of scrap paper. She smiled as she saw him coming.

Her warm voice rang out softly. *And here comes Mister Will with another word! God bless us all.* She saw the word and raised her hand to her mouth to hush a cry that would not have been at home in the Monticello town library.

### FIFTY-SIX

It was after supper a few days after Lennie went down to the draw. Ray was at his Optimists International meeting. Lennie called Will in from the back yard, where he was staring at the last rays of the sun. It was something of a ritual with him, she knew, and, like as not, Nici was there with him or else under that fig tree of hers. He came in willingly, curiously. She sat him down with a gesture, then unfolded her checkerboard on the delicate tablecloth she crocheted during the past several months. She produced the leather bag she found by the well. Will sat up, his eyes shining. Lennie emptied the bag on the board.

*Teach me*, she said to Will.

Will's hands flew to the board like white doves, and Lennie leaned toward her nephew, her glasses full of light.

## FIFTY-SEVEN

The next week at the library Will finished reading the very strange story of Oedipus the King and felt the bright wonder of ancient history flow over him. He wrote down larger words to look up in the *Webster's* at home. Most of them were smaller words forced together and obvious to him. Each word was a brick in the walls of the house, every book a house, the library a town of knowledge.

His father was late, and Will took out an encyclopedia and turned to *Monticello*. There in the encyclopedia he saw a miniature of a domed house on a hill in Virginia surrounded by gardens and sloping lawns. He read quicker and quicker, fearing his father's arrival.

Ray entered the library door and stopped there. He saw Will kneeling on a chair bent over a large tan book. *Will*, he whispered roughly from where he was.

*Sh-h-h-h!* hissed Miss Jones at the desk. *This is a library, Mr. Falke.*

He walked over to the desk where Miss Jones was quietly stamping cards. *Is my boy being a bother?*

She studied the gruff man twice her age, a Professor of Industrial Education at the nearby college. *No bother*, she said. *No bother at all. He read the old Jefferson book you gave us some time ago. Now he's looking up words he doesn't understand.*

Ray remembered the first time he had met this young woman. It was over two years ago, when she first came. It was shortly after Will returned from Little Rock and before Ruth's trouble became such a concern. It was on a Saturday afternoon, very much like this one. Will was over there then, in the same area, staring down at a red book.

*What's he doing over there?* Ray asked, his brow furrowed.

*He's reading the Encyclopedia Britannica, Mr. Falke.*

*Hm-m-m-m*, Ray murmured, shaking his head slightly.

*The boy's four, right?* she asked.

*What?* said Ray, distracted by a large blue fly that came in with him. *Is he a problem?*

Miss Jones studied him a moment, without judgment.

*You've got a four-year-old reading the Encyclopedia Britannica and you ask me if he's a problem? I'd say he's both a problem and a blessing, all things being equal, which they never seem to be.* She studied Ray, who avoided her gaze, and then she added, *I thought you might be proud.*

*He'll be five next week*, Ray said.

He thanked Miss Jones for a second time, strode over to Will, tapped his shoulder and started toward the door.

Miss Jones waited for Will's smile to flash at her from the doorway before she left her desk to put the encyclopedia back on its shelf.


### FIFTY-EIGHT

In the library, Will often saw a small, slight man poring over books in the music section. Strange, he always seemed to wear his hat, a neat dark hat. Once Will saw one of the older librarians nod toward Mr. Gold and whisper the word he had once heard his father spit out like a curse. *Jew.* What did it mean?

The librarian said he made her uneasy, no matter how often he came. She could never get used to him. She whispered, *The Jew tucks his tail in his pants, hides his horns under his hat.*

Will was struck dumb by the image. One Saturday, when it was nearly time to meet his father at the feed store, Will followed Mr. Gold away from the library with hopes that the wind would blow Mr. Gold's small, dark hat from his head. Then he would see. Unfortunately, there was very little wind that Saturday.

They neared an old apartment building, surrounded by untrimmed evergreens. The yellow bricks of the building and the poorly watered grass were nearly the same color. The old man paused at the end of the city sidewalk before turning up the ten feet of broken concrete to the door of the apartment building. Will also hesitated, then as the old man went slowly to his door, Will followed to where the old man left the sidewalk. When he heard the man's voice, dry and crisp as an autumn leaf, Will was strangely calm. Mr. Gold turned slightly and Will saw the smooth pink of a clean-shaven cheek.

*So, does he want to come in?* The voice was slight and musical in a way that Will had never heard. Without hesitation, Will moved toward the old man, who entered the doorway before him, but hesitated inside to hold the door for the boy.

Will followed him inside the building and down a musty hallway to a green door at the end. Inside the apartment was a different world from any Will had ever known. Every wall was lined with books from top to bottom. There were large books lying on big shelves at the bottom. Will knew those books contained maps, and he longed to open them

*Sit.* The old man gestured to a plain wooden chair near a low ornate table of shiny black wood. Will did not move. *Sit*, he insisted, his voice increasingly warm. *Sit*. And Will did.

*You like music?*

Will nodded yes.

*Good. It's good to like music.* And he picked a record from among the furthermost shelves, set it carefully on an old Victrola, turned the machine on, slowly raised the arm of the machine, then ever-so-slowly settled the needle on the platter. *This is one of an old man's favorites.* He moved over to the window, opened the blind a little, and gazed out on the yellow lawn.

There was static like dry wind in weeds, but the music was clear. Woodwinds called plaintively like a bird call far off. Then a warm, dark voice began to sing phrase after phrase of pulsing song. Will slowly leaned back in the chair and surrendered to the music's hypnotic power. Near the end, there was a pause, then a great, beautiful cry that left him breathless and in tears.

Mr. Gold gazed at him a moment from the window, then said, *I see, young man, that you understand music.* He turned to the Victrola, raised the arm carefully, and returned the album to its cover. On the cover was the engraving of a full-faced man with dark eyes and fine lips. *That was Caruso*, he said, raising the album. *About him, one can only...* He paused a moment, winked at Will, and raised his hat from his head in a salute to the album cover. Beneath his hat, Will saw a perfect eggshell head with a very little fringe about large ears.

Will knew it could not be true.

*You are relieved, yes?* Mr. Gold asked, his hat poised curiously above his head. *I wear it, well, in part, to protect what little is left of my brain after...* He paused in a most curious and thoughtful fashion, as if he did not know what he himself was going to say. Finally, a single word came out: *Europe*. Mr. Gold set the Caruso album aside and thoughtfully chose another. *And then there is the law.* He took the record from the cover and placed it on the machine.

*The law of hats?* asked Will, a little confused but very interested.

Mr. Gold looked at Will with delight, then answered with a gentle glee, *No, laws of the head. That is, laws for keeping the head covered, as a sign of always... remembering what is most important.*

*And what is that?* asked Will.

*My, my, my,* said Mr. Gold, raising the arm of the Victrola. *So many questions.* Then he raised the arm of the machine and let the record revolve in silence. He turned to Will. *More of hats later. But I have something else for you now. Yes, I want you to hear it. This music I play for you, it is opera—drama with music?* He looked at Will for recognition and saw none. *Like a film or television, yes?* Will nodded, slowly, unsure. He had seen television infrequently, at his friend Wayne's house. *But with living people singing with an orchestra. You know the orchestra?*

Will sat up, suddenly excited. *Yes,* he said. *Strings from Italy, winds from France, brass from Germany.*

*Wheee!* sang out the old man, and tossed his hat as high as the low ceiling would allow. He caught his hat with one hand and placed it slanted on his head. *He's alive, he knows something!*

Will giggled and drew his knees up to his chin on the old chair, which creaked appreciatively.

*Let me tell you something more!* He paused and studied Will. *What is your name, my lad?*

*Will.*

*So, it is William, yes?*

*Yes.*

*So, William, I will call you Wolf. It is good? I like it very much that a wolf followed me home today and is here with me.* He laughed softly to himself. *Now how will I ever keep you from my door?* He laughed again, at Will's curious stare. *Such a wolf!* His eyes grew large, playful.

*Okay,* said Will, *but I don't see why you don't call me Will.*

*Some day I will tell you, my dear Wolf. In the meantime, let me tell you something more. This piece I will play for you is called an aria. It's a special kind of song. Do you wish to know about them?* He gazed at Will as his mother had.

*Yes, I would,* said Will, and he had never said more sincere words.

*An aria is a poem written to be sung, not spoken. Usually, it tells everything about the person who sings it. It is about the singer's heart and soul. And not just the words that are important. The words are, in fact, but the beginning of the aria's meaning, like a sketch of an oil painting. The words represent thought, but the music represents emotion.* He walked slowly to the window, gazing outward. *Music represents the heart, yes, and maybe the soul sometimes.* He inserted two fingers into the blind and opened the slit wider next to his face. His sharp prominent nose disappeared as his bright green eyes turned to Will. *The aria you heard before is sung by an old man*—he paused and winked at Will—*like me.* His expression became more serious, and his eyes never left Will's. *He has many problems, problems which need not concern a young man like you.* He paused and returned to the machine. *Now, for something else entirely. I will say a few words to introduce a young woman to you. Her name is Lucia, but people call her Mimi. She pretends to be happy but is really terribly afraid of being alone. She is, you see, very sick. But never mind. In this aria—you know the word now, yes—she tells a new friend what she does. She embroiders—*

*Like Aunt Lennie!* Will interjected.

*Yes, possibly*, said Mr. Gold, an amused smile cracking his face, *but not unless your Aunt Lennie lived in Paris a hundred years ago.*

*No*, said Will, *she lives in Hopkinsville, Kentucky. Anyway, she makes quilts and doilies.*

*I see*, said Mr. Gold, amused at Will's verbosity. *But may I continue?*

*She's living with us while my mother's away in Little Rock having an operation*, said Will. *She makes cinnamon rolls for breakfast.*

*Ah, yes. I'm sure she does*, said Mr. Gold patiently, and sat down near Will.

How long Will talked or what he said Will himself never entirely remembered, but when he ceased he was looking into the wide eyes of Mr. Gold. Will stopped speaking and gazed open-mouthed into the kindly glow of the old man's face.

*I see*, said Mr. Gold. *You are a most interesting young man.* He stood up. *May I play* mi chiamo mimi *for you now?*

*Yes, please*, said Will, shaking his head slightly in wonder at Mr. Gold's words and, more, the careful and precise way in which the older man honored him with what Will sensed was something important.

*Good, my dear Wolf, because I am quite sure that we both have places to go and things to do on a Saturday evening.* He hesitated, then said thoughtfully. *Let me only say this about arias. You will understand later. I think you remember words very clearly, yes? Good, it is a gift. An aria is a lyric poem set to transcendently beautiful music for orchestra and voice. The voice represents words as thought, while the music, especially the vocal melody represents the emotions— but together, Wolf, together they express the world inside a person as nothing else can.* Here, he raised his slender hands and enfolded the fingers. *The aria is a special truth about special people—characters— who may live forever. These are the words of a simple girl with the soul of an angel.* He paused, then added thoughtfully, *Rather like your Miss Jones in the library, no? She is the one not so worried about silly things like tails and horns. She is more worried about little boys who miss their mothers, yes?*

Will leaned back in his chair.

Mr. Gold played the aria, and Will entered into the ecstasy of music he had never dreamed existed. He rose and fell with the lovely voice and his heart flew about in his chest like a wild bird. He felt his mother at his side for the first time in months. He sat stunned after the music ceased.

*Like the aria, Mimi is simple to experience, but very complex to know well,* said Mr. Gold. *Now, you better hurry away, little bird.*

Will was never the same after that day.

Will met his father over an hour late at the feed store. Ray was angry at the delay, but he was too tired for a trip to the stump. Besides, there was such a glow about the boy that Ray was reminded of Ruth. He listened to his son's humming—like the wind in the trees, he thought—on the way home and said nothing.

### FIFTY-NINE

Will studied Lennie's face as she read from the family Bible. The little room was dark and quiet. She read by moonlight, facing the window. There was a gaunt beauty about her face, softened as it was by the moonlight. He knew this light, even this arrangement of the things he beheld. Miss Jones had explained it to him one day when she found him with an oversized book, *The Great Dutch Painters.* It was the picture of a woman reading a letter by light coming from a window on the left. There was a map in the background—very clear, like his map of Arkansas on the wall behind his aunt, whose severe profile glowed warmly with moonlight.

Lennie read plainly, her voice twanging with each *n* and *ng* of the poetry. Occasionally, her loose fitting dentures clicked, creating a different kind of music that Will had grown to love through the months of her reading to him at bedtime. Certain words caught him by surprise.

*Wait,* he whispered. *Please read that again.*

*Which part?* asked Lennie, shaken from a reverie of sorts.

*About the hawk*, said the boy, now sitting up in the bed.

Lennie found the place with an impossibly long, narrow finger.

*Is it through your wisdom*
*That the hawk grows pinions*
*And spreads its wings to the south?*

*Oh, wonderful!* whispered Will, and fell back on the bed. He relaxed, closed his eyes, and within two additional verses was asleep.

Lennie stood and gazed at her nephew. His head rested uneasily on the thin pillow. She saw there her brother's pale face before his death, then her father's, and then a hundred patients she nursed toward their end. She had accepted the death of many in her life and in her profession. She reached down shyly, not given to grace, and ran her hand through the fine hair above his ear. She embraced the mystery of love as, deep in sleep, Will murmured in tongues. And it seemed to her as if his head reached up to meet her touch.

## SIXTY

Will and Nici lay on the slanting, still-warm tin roof, unaccustomed shoes toward the setting sun, vermilion and pale purple in its last quiet statement. They lay, side by side, her head resting on his sleeve. She shivered. It was early December, and they were bundled against the cold evening.

*Mommy comes home soon*, said Will.

*Yep*, murmured Nici, snuggling against her big brother—a little like his first dog used to, Will thought.

*Daddy says she's changed*, Will added, after a pause.

*Changed how?* said Nici, putting her right hand flat on the tin roof for warmth.

*He didn't say*, said Will, *but I saw her…*

*When did you see her? Where?* blurted out Nici, suddenly awake. It was eight months since Ruth disappeared in a cloud of the '49 Pontiac's dust. *Well?* She sat up.

Will glanced at her, then stared at the place on the horizon to the left of the pine, where the sun had gone down.

*I don't know. I heard him telling Aunt Lennie that the doctors said the quicker she comes home the better. She needs a real long time to get better. No one knows how long. But she needs to be home with us.*

*Well*, said Nici thoughtfully, *maybe we can help.*

*Yeah*, said Will, *I think that's what the doctors want. I just think she may be different, changed from what she was before.*

*That's okay, as long as she comes back.* Nici grew quiet, studied her brother. *You said you saw her, right?*

Will looked at her, trustingly. *Yes, I did.*

*So what did you see?*

*It was in a dream.*

*Oh goody, I love dreams.*

*Only this one wasn't so good.*

Nici lay back on the cooling tin.

*Mom was like an angel, all in white. Hospitals are full of white and silver stuff. I saw her in a bed. She was skinny and pale and seemed unhappy there.*

*Maybe because she wants to be here with us,* said Nici.

Will laughed softly, *Yep, I bet you're right. That's it.*

Nici snuggled closer. *Yep, that's it.*

Gray evening was closing around them.

*You know what I was scared of?* Nici suddenly whispered.

*No,* answered Will. *What?*

*That she might come back different, you know, really weird—like you!*

With these last two words, she giggled and rolled away from him, her slender form disappearing over the edge of the roof. Chagrined for not having seen it coming, Will caught up with her by leaping from the roof, just as she left the lowest rung of the ragged board fence that served as their ladder. He landed, grabbed her, and pinned her to the ground.

*What do you mean, weird like me?* Will roared in mock rage.

*Oh, it's you,* she said laughing up at Will. *I thought it was a big chicken.*

*Weird? A chicken? Do you have any idea of what I could do to you?*

*Not much,* said Nici, giggling. Then, she smiled up at Will's sunset face. *Anyway, if Mom's no weirder than you, I guess it'll be okay.*

*Well,* said Will, rolling off Nici into the cool grass and shivering with the damp moisture. *Little Rock is not a good place.*

*Okay, Mr. Will,* she said. He playfully took her head in the crook of his arm and squeezed her close. She giggled her high musical laugh and said, *Bony! Eeek! My brother is boneeeeeey.*

Together they wrestled and laughed away the remaining light, there on the cold ground beneath the rusted tin bed of the sky.

# PART THREE
**Winter 1952/Spring 1953**


In ragged fronts, storms crossed in: early moon
Furrowed by cloudbanks—cat eye in comet road.
God's pocked eye shone in my father's storm,
Its light pierced leaves as they slept—they rustled.
He paused at soft thunder, glanced up restive,
Then pointed where a spine of stratus arched the sky,
*See it fly now!* He said. And, masts bending,
Massive trees caught wind, their true forms first clear.
Rain approached in lines, then masses from the broken vault,
And with electric steps I reeled along the path,
Out of the dark wood, along open fields—
Over those dry clay spaces, I danced with lightning.
Under torn skies, I ran unbridled toward
Gates where Father still strides on before me.

## SIXTY-ONE

The sleek bulk of the 1949 Pontiac crept from the empty road up the driveway until it rested before the house's slight wire fence. The slanting gate so difficult to keep closed was ajar, and the broken strip of walkway that led to the concrete steps and solid front porch of the house glinted dully in mid-afternoon sunlight. In the shade on the front porch, in front of the doorway to the warm living room, a quartet of restless children gathered. They watched Lennie's angular frame descend the front steps to wait by the gate as the dust drifted by the car. Then, as Ray's door opened, she went to the passenger door and opened it. Her eyes—so accustomed to hospitals, recovery rooms, and long lingering descents—grew large and clouded as she studied the rangy child sprawled in the front seat. Her gaze was not returned, for Ruth's face was buried in a quilt. Lennie felt cold in the bright sun. Where was the vivacious girl who bore five children under her watchful eye? Nothing in her experience led her to expect this frail, crumpled form. Then her brother was beside her, and she moved aside for him.

Will crept down from the front porch and watched his father carefully lift the folded bundle from the front seat. On Ray's left shoulder, Will saw a pale face beneath a blue stocking-hat. Dangling near his father's waist, a pair of bony legs descended to his mother's blue slippers. Will moved down the stairs to the sidewalk and realized as he did that Nici accompanied him like a shadow.

As his father passed Will and Nici, one of the slippers fell off, and Will saw his mother's foot, pale and beautiful in the mid-winter light, its ivory and light blue shadows startlingly clear for a long moment. He retrieved the slipper and covered the foot before his father was much delayed. He and Nici followed him up the steps and entered the warmth of the house where a strong wood fire was burning. Ray paused only slightly as he passed close between Judith and Barbara, then went directly to the bedroom. Lennie followed him. The children gathered before the fireplace, glancing each to the other.

When Ray emerged from the bedroom, he looked at them a moment, then said, *Your mother is resting. The trip from Little Rock tired her out.*

Soon Lennie came out and sat close to them, stretching out her gaunt hands to the fireplace warmth. The coals glowed in her glasses. *I was there when each of you was born*, she said. *I saw what your mother went through for you. Now it's your turn.*

After dinner, Will helped Lennie with the dishes. Nici perched on the sink, her feet in the warm sudsy water. Later, after Nici was tucked in and while his father and Lennie whispered in the kitchen, Will crept in to his mother's bed. Finding her cold feet under Aunt Lennie's quilt, he held and massaged them until they were warm.

That day was February 13, Will's birthday.

That night, Will dreamed of a strange beast singing in their woods. He pursued it, but no matter how hard he searched through the dense forest, it lingered just beyond sight. He saw clearly, however, the shadowy figure of another child, one his age, and this child, he knew, had seen the creature he sought.

### SIXTY-TWO

On the rare days Will missed the school bus home, it was because he was mopping the auditorium at Drew Central Grade School. That was the punishment for breaking a classroom rule. It was, of course, nothing compared to the inevitable second punishment that waited for him at home. The principal called home, and Ray took Will to the stump.

When Will broke a classroom rule, it was almost always because a classmate teased him about his eyes. The transgression that occurred a week after Ruth's return, however, was different. During the afternoon recess, Will remained in Mrs. Webb's homeroom to complete his homework. As he completed the math assignment, he was startled to see a cloud of tiny particles drifting down onto the lined paper and settling on his hands. Then, he heard a snigger behind him and turned to see TJ Johnson rubbing two erasers together just above his head. Cleaning erasers was a classroom punishment for minor offenses such as belching or farting in class. TJ was an expert in the latter category of expression.

Will whirled to face the skinny rooster. *Why, you little...* Will uttered and rushed him.

TJ's eyes grew large as he backed away from the spare desk piled high with dusty erasers. He ran toward the door, then promptly veered away from it after glancing through it. As TJ swerved abruptly toward Mrs. Webb's desk and the possibility of freedom out one of the large, half-open windows that opened out onto the playground, Will's arm cocked back, an eraser grasped firmly between his thumb and index finger. As TJ ran past the desk toward the windows, erasers began bouncing off his back. Giggling, he caught one and threw it back. Ten erasers were in play before the principal's head appeared in the doorway to call out sternly, *Cease fire!*

Mr. Stoddard's words caught Will in mid-downstroke. Being blind in his right eye, he had no idea the principal was there until the voice rang out. So Will's last projectile left his hand ever so slightly after the commander's order to cease fire sounded. That last eraser caught the stationary TJ squarely on the nose, producing a loud yelp and a considerable cloud of chalk dust. This struck Will as momentarily hilarious and as he and TJ exchanged glances, they both burst out laughing. TJ stopped first, because his face, white with chalk dust, was beginning to feature a bright red dot beneath its nostrils.

Then Will crouched down, trying to stifle his laughter, holding his head in his hands. He heard TJ snigger once, blow his nose, and begin to snuffle. Then he saw Mr. Stoddard's wing tips filling the floor in front of him.

*Well, boys, I must say*, remarked the principal not unkindly, *you two have certainly discovered a unique method of cleaning erasers.* His voice seemed to smile, Will thought, though everyone knew how stern he was. His whippings were notorious among the older boys. He was a large, powerful man. He had been in the war. He generally stood straight and moved across the stage or playground with a broad rhythmic movement that Will found beautiful. It was as if he were defining the space around him with the regular motion of his arms and legs in combination. His voice continued, deep and resonant.

*TJ, I know you have a long bus ride home and are needed for work there, so you will have the honor of cleaning the auditorium tomorrow at noon. If you finish quickly, you may have time to eat your lunch afterwards.* He turned to look down at Will. *You, Sir, will polish every board in that auditorium floor today immediately after school.* He paused and studied something out the window. *TJ, I will be calling your family about this.* TJ smiled, knowing that there would be little if any consequence. There might even be slight praise. *And, Will, despite your potential to become the next Bob Feller, I will be calling your house as well.*

Will caught his breath lightly, which did not escape the principal. He had seen Will limp into school the days after he called Ray Falke in the past. But rules were rules.

## SIXTY-THREE

Will was halfway finished arranging the chairs on the west side of the auditorium when he became aware of the brown-clad figure of Mrs. Webb watching him from near the stage steps. Whatever her reason, he was grateful for the company in the vast empty room. He pushed the large mop nearer to her.

*So, William,* she said softly, her voice shimmering in the wooden spaces that confined them, *I understand your mother has come home from Little Rock.*

*Yes, ma'am,* Will said.

*You must be happy to see her.*

*Yes, ma'am, I am.*

*Well, William, forgive me for saying this, but you don't seem very happy. I know it's none of my business, but is everything all right?*

*Yes, ma'am,* he said, turning back to his work. Then he added, without thinking, *Maybe.*

*Maybe, Will?*

Will stared into the emptiness in the rear of the auditorium, his voice echoing slightly, so that Mrs. Webb struggled to understand him. *She's like my mother, only it's not really her.*

*Why Will, whatever do you mean?*

*Her hair is gone,* he said, slowly turning to her. *You know my mother's hair, like sunset, all reddish bright?* Her heart leapt at his words. *It's all gone. And she just sits, doesn't talk or sing. Aunt Lennie takes care of us. She's real good, especially with my sisters. It's just that my mom sits and stares at us like we were strangers. We show her family books, you know, like snapshots, but she doesn't seem to know anyone. She doesn't even know us. She can't even eat by herself. We feed her.* He made a slight, indescribable gesture with his hands. *You see? No hair, no song, no Mom.* He paused and grabbed the mop handle like an unwieldy broad sword. *It was better before, even with the fits. At least there was someone I knew there.* Mrs. Webb caught herself up and searched in her purse for something. Will returned to his work, saying, *I have to finish now. My father will be waiting for me.*

*Yes, he will,* thought Mrs. Webb, *with his belt or whatever he used. Will,* she said, *I will see you tomorrow.*

*Yes, ma'am,* Will said and attacked the east side of the auditorium.

## SIXTY-FOUR

As Will walked past the college tennis courts an hour later, he heard a slight whimper from the ditch beside the road. He saw a lumpy burlap bag in a shallow puddle of the recent rain. He pried open the baling wire that closed the sack a few inches down from its neck, and saw a brown puppy, its eyes newly opened and belly swollen with hunger. Will held it up and it managed, though trembling violently with cold in the afternoon sun, to feebly lick the boy once on his nose. Will put the pup back in the bag and slung it gently over his shoulder. As he headed for home into the early sunset, the pup snuggled into him. The pain of the scarlet sunset and his dread of his father waiting for him, razor strap in hand, were lessened by the warm bump on his back.

When he reached home, Will snuck around the side of the house to the garage and put the puppy in an empty tomato basket lined with a torn feedsack. Then he went to the house and followed his father out to the stump before chores. As he bent over and caught his ankles, he thought of taking the puppy some warm milk after milking.

## SIXTY-FIVE

*The River Jordan is muddy and cold*
*It chills the body but not the soul*

Late at night and long after the others were asleep, Lennie hummed her mother's tune as she went to her narrow bed just off the kitchen in the late-quiet home of her brother. She undressed simply, her form a study of plainness. She slipped her wool nightgown down over her short, tight curls and knelt beside her bed.

She prayed for the soul of her mother Elizabeth, who sang her to sleep in the brief years before the bloody cough claimed her. *How a voice so sweet could come from those poor lungs.* She prayed for Ted in his fierce recklessness, for Ruth in her wounded gentleness, for Barbara and Judith in their women's pain, for Will in his wrestling, for Nici—for Nici and Will, as they shaped the seed of something sweet between them that she and Ted never had but now struggled toward—that little angel. And, Dear God, for the family she had here and at home in Kentucky, the children she never had but was fighting for now, for the greater family and the circle of love it could bring around the wounded in their wrestling with evil. And for poor little Fred in Dry Fork, please God, Amen.

Suddenly, she was tired. As she rose, she smelled the pungent fragrance of cinnamon dough on her hands. She knew how Will loved them and she doted on him, just a little. She laid back the covers of the bed and smoothed the sheets. As she laid her head on the down pillow she always traveled with, she once again heard her mother's voice, as soft as a feather.

> *Hush, little baby, don't you cry*
> *You know your mother was born....*

Her last thought was that perhaps, somehow, Will might hear what she heard in that moment of whiteness, of falling back to what, in the moment of its birth, always seemed to hold the promise of endless peace. When that boy cried out at night, it not only tore her from sleep. It gnawed her soul.

## SIXTY-SIX

*This is your mother, Grandma Crooks*, Will said, placing his finger on the sepia image of a round-faced woman, her braids wound tightly about the sides of her head. The album rested on Ruth's knees. Nici was perched on the arm of the rocking chair, her feet in Ruth's lap and her slender arm about Ruth's neck. Ruth was delighted that the little girl rested her head against her cheek, moving it only occasionally to kiss Ruth or, echoing Will, to reach down and point a tiny dirty finger at a photograph in the book below. Will stood on his mother's right, leaning on the arm of the rocking chair, steadying the book in his mother's lap. It was a Sunday morning in March, sunny and chilly. Since her return Ruth was happiest in the rocker near the sewing machine when the late morning sun shone brightly into the house.

*Gamma Coogs*, mumbled Ruth, with effort.

Nici giggled. *No, Mommy. Granma Crooks. It's your mommy!*

*Yu monny*, murmured Ruth, looking up at Nici.

*No, no*, said Nici, kissing her mother repeatedly as she spoke. *No. You're my mommy. That's your mommy.* Then she giggled again, a high sweet sound.

Ruth smiled, looking at Will, blankly. She seemed to have weakened in just the last few moments. Will placed his hands on his mother's shoulders. *My mommy*, he said, grasping the lean corners of her body. Then he turned in the book to a large, sepia photograph of Ruth and Ray taken on their wedding day. Their smiles were full, their eyes bright. *This is my mommy. This is you, Ruth Jean Crooks Falke.* He turned back to the photograph of Grandma Crooks. *And this is your mommy.* He pointed at Grandma Crooks: *Your mommy.* And back to the wedding picture, *My mommy.* Each time he named his mother, he squeezed her shoulder, with his left hand. Point and squeeze, point and squeeze. *You. My mommy. You, my mommy. You are my mommy.* As he did so, he remembered Tyree's vast hands enclosing his own shoulders, as he tried to help Will with his problems. Down by the well that failed.

Ruth smiled weakly and said, *My mommy*, staring at Will's finger resting on her own photograph. Will felt a strange coldness about his heart. His eyes fell.

Ruth studied the silent boy beside her, and then she made a little gesture with her hand. *Turn the page.* Will raised his eyes to study his mother's face, to make sure he was true to her will. Then he turned back to the sepia print of Grandma Crooks. Ruth studied it only a moment before she said, *My mommy*, and placed her hand unsteadily on Will's pointing finger.

Nici giggled and kissed her mother excitedly on the cheek.

*Yes, Good!* said Will.

He took Ruth's hand, placed it on his chest. *Your son.* Ruth's eyes rested on him. He moved her hand to Nici's head. *Your daughter.*

Ruth slowly moved her hand back to Will's chest. Her mouth dry, her jaw shaking, she murmured, *Mah son.*

An electric shock stunned Will. Nici stared at her mother. Will stared into his mother's eyes and said, *My son, Will.* Ruth made a small gesture with both hands and, trembling, she said, so softly that Will was not sure at first that he had actually heard it. *Mah son, Will.*

Will embraced his mother. Nici laughed delightedly and clapped her hands. Ruth closed her eyes and was truly happy as she could not remember being. It must have been a very long time.

And Ruth fell back exhausted.

## SIXTY-SEVEN

Kay Griner drove her toe shyly into a crack in the sidewalk and then turned it there slowly. She looked steadily at Will, and he smiled to himself. It was as if she were two people, the nervous one whose leg twisted beneath her, and the serious, bright-eyed girl who confronted him with her stare whenever they were together. It was April, a crisp and bright afternoon. The playground was a pale green. They were standing on the broken sidewalk on the west side of the school, near the path that led from the school to Kay's house on Lakeshore Drive. He first met Kay when he lived on the other end of the Drive; that was three years ago.

*Are you coming to my birthday party on Sunday or not, Will Falke?* she asked, her leg moving beneath her cotton dress. She wore a new pink jacket over the dress and both garments hung from her spare frame and moved easily in the sharp breeze. They sometimes met right after school and talked. It was an unspoken agreement. They were, he guessed, friends.

*I forgot to ask if I could*, he said. He was lying and she knew it. Birthday parties were something unquestioned among children. Only extreme punishment kept a kid away. He was afraid and she knew it.

*There you go, Will. You're wandering off as you listen. I swear you can't just listen to a person without drifting off somewhere. You're not the easiest person in the world to talk to, you know that?* Her leg finally stopped moving, and she anchored her arms akimbo at her waist.

*Now she looks like my mother does, when she's angry*, thought Will. And he smiled.

*And now I guess you're laughing at me, too.* She paused, relieved to have a verbal outlet for the tension she felt when she was around Will. *Do you want me to slap you right upside the head?*

*Yes, please.* The words were out of Will's mouth before he knew it.

She screamed with laughter and drew back her hand in mock outrage.

He ran and she pursued. He ran just fast enough to evade her until he wanted to be caught, then shielded himself as best he could from her comic flailing. Neither could stop giggling for a while. Then she drew away and studied him. He was laughing, but tears streamed down his face, and he did not seem to be able to stop. She moved back close to him. Gradually he relaxed, but his breath remained a strong pulse against her and still he could not stop crying softly.

Then, his eyes locked hers. When he stared at her in that way, she hardly noticed what everyone, even her mother, remarked about—his eyes. She felt tears in her own eyes.

How her arms came to be around him neither of them knew, but Will finally stopped crying in their narrow radius.

Kay drew back again from him and held him at arm's length. *Do you want my mama to call your mama?* she asked, wiping her eyes unselfconsciously.

He nodded. *I just never know when my dad may need me*, he said. *And when he needs me, I have to be there.*

She studied him a brief moment. *Well, I hope he doesn't need you Sunday from one till four*, she said, and added with a twinkle, *cause we do!* And her leg began its dance again.

In that moment, she seemed to Will the most graceful of all things. Her extended leg seemed full of a meaning he could not grasp. Her smile and eyes were bright in the dappled sunlight. Her soft giggle was music.

## SIXTY-EIGHT

The garage was a dusty storage place, and Ray entered it infrequently in winter. He entered it one early spring evening, however, searching for a sawhorse, and there he found Will and Nici playing quietly with the puppy, which was fat and sleek from fresh milk twice a day and a snuck-out portion of Will's supper, chewed up real fine. Ray was furious.

*How long?* he demanded.

Will pulled the pup into his lap. *About a month*, he said. *I found him in a bag by the tennis courts. He was thrown away.*

*Well, why didn't you leave it there? Damn it, Will, we don't need another mouth to feed around here.*

*Please, Papa. He won't be any trouble. I'll take care of him myself.*

*Oh, you will?! Well, that's just fine. And who do you think takes care of you, feeds you and breaks his goddamned back every day to put food on the table?* He stared at the boy hugging the puppy, his youngest daughter's wide eyes studying him with a curious calm. *I don't want it here.*

*Papa, please.*

*Will, god damn it!*

*He's a good dog*, Will whispered. *He never hurt anybody.*

*You're whining just like that damned mutt*, Ray said. *Get rid of it, or I will.*

Will watched the garage door vibrate on its hinges after his father's exit.

*I'll do it*, he thought. *You won't.*

*But what will I do?* thought Will on the way to school the next day. *Where can I hide it?* All day long, he tried to give away the dog he found in the ditch. No one wanted it. Kay Griner had two dogs, one old, one young. She went home at lunch to ask, and returned to sniff, *We got two. That's enough for us, Mom says.* It was a long day of searching.

### SIXTY-NINE

Will emerged from the woods and approached Tyree's house. It was early evening. He called out into the house, *Tyree, you home?*

*I'm here all right*, came the deep voice from behind the house. And Tyree appeared from behind the house, torn overalls stretched over his immense frame. Josh was with him. *Why, Will boy, this a surprise. What you got there?*

Before Will could answer, Josh was there, roughing the puppy's ears gently and asking to hold it. Will surrendered the puppy to Josh's strong hands.

*Hey, Josh*, said Will.

*Hey, Will*, he answered, smiling as the puppy licked the dust from his face.

*Hey, Mr. Will*, said Tyree. *We fixing to eat now. Why don't you boys sit on the porch and I'll bring you out some. It ain't much, some greens and fatback.* And he disappeared into the house, his rich voice singing after him, *But it sho keep the growls away.*

When each was wolfing down a plate of salted greens and fatback, Tyree spoke. *So how you doing since I filled up that big old hole we done dug in the draw?*

*Not so good*, said Will.

*M-m-m-m*, hummed Joshua as he nuzzled the dog and gave it a very small piece of the fatback. It was a melody that sounded familiar to Will, but he couldn't name it.

*Yo mother done come back home?*

*Yes.*

*How she doing?*

*Okay, maybe, but she doesn't remember me.*

*Well, I'll be.* Tyree studied Will, then took a long drink of well water from the dipper. *Joshua*, he said, *maybe you could fetch us another dip of that good well water.*

*Sho, Daddy*, said Joshua. *Will, I'm going to take your dog. Okay?*

*Okay, Josh,* said Will. And Josh was gone.

*M- m- m- m,* said Tyree thoughtfully. *She don't know you, huh?*
*Nope, not really.*
*My, my. Well, she gonna need some time to get to know you again, ain't she?*
*What you mean, Tyree?*
*I mean, imagine how she must feel, poor lady, coming home to a house full of people and knowing no one. Must be hard for her.* Tyree sat on the porch, which groaned loudly.
*Yeah, I guess.*
*You gonna help her, ain't you?*
*Yes, we are all going to do that.* Will was surprised to feel tears on his cheeks. *Tyree, I got a new mother.*
*Yeh, I see that, Honey.*
*But I liked the old one, Tyree. I want her back.*

Tyree took Will in his arms. As he did so, Tyree felt the cold dipper against his arm. Josh had returned, the puppy slung over his shoulder. Tyree clapped Will softly on the back and placed the boy beside him on the porch.

Will remembered why he came. *Tyree, can you and Josh keep this puppy? Daddy says I have to get rid of it.*
*H-m—m-m-m,* hummed Tyree, glancing over at Josh.
*I'll come get him back later,* said Will. *At least, I think I can.*
*What do you say, Josh?* said Tyree. *Do we need another one?*
Josh smiled broadly in a way that gave his father joy.
*Well, sure then, Will. We'll look after him for a little while.*
*Thanks.*
*You welcome, you truly welcome.*

After they finished their plates, Will danced with Tyree and Josh for the first time. Tyree put an old radio up in the window of the house and strutted over to the wagon where the boys sat petting the dogs. The sight of the huge man so enlivened by the sweet harmonies delighted the boys. Joshua sprang up on the wagon and began moving easily to the arching rhythms. Unthinking, Will jumped up beside him and joined Joshua's dance in his own way. Tyree observed them with satisfaction and urged them on with soft clapping. He slipped off his brogans to feel the cool dust between his toes as he swayed and pranced in the evening light beside the wagon.

The words of the song echoed in Will's ears on the pathway home. There was only the coolness on his chest where the puppy had been two hours before to remind him of what had sent him west to Tyree's and what awaited him at home.

## SEVENTY

The puppy easily freed itself from Joshua's sleeping grasp and, finding in the unusual easterly breeze a slight acrid sweetness, trotted across the clearing containing Tyree's house, sheds, and wagon and entered the shade of the woods. It found there the old path, worn deep in the earth and rich with scents. Among these scents was the sweet smell of boy and boy sweat that was associated with warm milk and tumbling blindly among feed sacks.

The barbed wire fence between the Falke fifty acres and Tyree's sharecrop presented no problem. The pup trotted under the lowest strand. Had it been weeks older and had the lower strand caught his smooth back and drawn blood, it would hardly have noticed. So strong was the pull of the children and warm milk on its slight soul.

It emerged from the woods and started across the large warm field. A hundred yards later, it entered the shade of the pine and there experienced a thrill of familiarity. The boy's scent was powerful here. He sniffed excitedly around the tree. The boy was not there but had been recently.

Then came the greatest challenge: the field between the tree and the house had recently been plowed. The puppy sniffed the southeasterly breeze and found a faint tinge of the boy there. He trotted into the rough furrows, following the trace toward the farmhouse and garage.

The furrows were deep and rough and threatened to enclose the slight dog entirely, but the pull of the broken earth was not strong enough yet. The puppy entered the back yard through the gate's slant. Exhausted, it managed to lap a little water from the cistern rope before slipping into the garage. Seeing no child there, it fell asleep immediately in its tomato basket.

Nici found him later that day. Will was overjoyed to see him, but frightened because he had told his father days before that *it was all taken care of.*

## SEVENTY-ONE

That day on the bus home Will wanted to sit close to the front, but wound up about half-way back on the right, behind poor Joyce Causey. Joyce was left-handed but was forced by her parents and teachers to use her right hand in school. Her right hand trembled as she struggled to form her large rounded letters. She was a very quiet girl, almost always alone. *High strung*, people said. Will saw her run only once, on the playground, to retrieve an assignment the wind grabbed and carried away. She ran after it like an old person, all stiff, crying out. He heard rumors about her older parents and the way arthritis caused her joints to stiffen and ache. She gazed steadily out the window as the bus left the schoolyard. *At least she's a girl*, Will thought, *so they leave her alone*. Then he heard the little cry within himself, the small voice singing out, *You can't know what she goes through at home, in bed, in her dream*s.

Will felt a tap on his left shoulder. As he turned, he heard the high giggle of Jimmy White's girlfriend. She was famous for offering her seat in Jimmy's car to *anyone who was big enough to take it*. For some reason, this gave her some kind of special power and, at the same time, made Jimmy beam whenever she said it. Will didn't understand but liked Jimmy, who was the best cotton picker in the area. Jimmy's aged parents spent most of the day in their rockers. Before the last meanness on the bus, Jimmy had always been nice to Will.

Jimmy tapped Will's left shoulder again. Will did not turn. He remembered Jimmy's trick from before. It was painful, not so much because of the cut Jimmy's fingernail left beside his good eye but because it was Jimmy, and because it occurred to him for the first time that he might lose his good eye and be blind forever. That terrible thought passed through him and he shuddered.

Will did not turn and heard Jimmy scold his girl, who had given him away. She giggled and whispered a phrase built on the word *stupid* that Will could not understand. There was a pause, and Will wondered why Jimmy, who was eighteen and owned his own Chevy, would bother with him, the second-grader who lived around the corner and down the road. Why? Again Jimmy tapped Will's right shoulder. Will froze, then lowered his head.

*Billy Boy!* Jimmy's soft sing-song drifted through the bus. Will was still. *Oh, Billy Boy.*

The bus was silent, as it went past the tennis courts, and Will saw the dusty blackberry briars along the ditch where he'd found the puppy. In front of him, Joyce Causey stirred and stared hard out the dirty bus window.

*I'm telling you, Jimmy Smith*, a shrill voice behind Will

intoned. *That boy don't give you no respect. I don't like it at all.*

Will felt her small, strong hand on his head. First, it pushed his head farther down.

Will cried out, *Don't. That hurts.*

There was some laughter on the bus. *No shit, Sherlock*, said Jimmy. Jimmy's girl rose to her feet over Will and slapped him hard on the side of his head. Will jerked up at the pain, but Jimmy was suddenly beside him on the seat, pushing him against the side of the bus. Jimmy's voice was sharp, metallic.

*So you're a tough guy, huh? I heard about your big fight by the candy store. You're a big tough guy, aren't you?* He slapped Will, then rabbit punched him hard in the ribs. *Well, I'm going to kick your ass, you little cross-eyed piece of shit.* He grasped the back of Will's slender neck in his large, rough hand. The bully's hold, Will called it to himself when he saw it on the playground. Will heard the girl whisper instructions to Jimmy as she bent down over the seat. *That's it*, she whispered, *beat his ass. Hurt that boy!* Will had seen this happen to others; now it was his turn. Will struggled, but it was useless. His neck was in a vice, forced down between his legs. Her hand grabbed at him, pulled his hair. It felt like fire where she pulled.

The bus stopped across from Mrs. Stubblefield's place and some kids from the front of the bus got off quickly. *But this is Jimmy's stop.* Will impulsively turned to remind him, but as he did so Jimmy tightened his grip. Will felt his neck creak. He felt oddly sick.

Then Will heard another voice, darker and lower. Lewis Lamar moved in from the back of the bus. *Hey there, Jimmy boy*, said Lewis, *what'er you up to? You can't have all the fun by yourself.* Then he slapped Will hard on the back, sniggered, bent down, and whispered, *Those were friends of mine you hurt.* He said something in Jimmy's ear. As Jimmy laughed and nodded, the bus pulled away. It was not a quarter mile to Will's stop. He had to get off the bus, he couldn't stay on it—they had to let him go. His sisters would help him. Someone would help him.

Then Jimmy pulled Will out into the aisle. Lewis was between the driver and Will, while Jimmy and his girl held and slapped Will on the head and back.

*Let's see what this boy has between his legs*, said Lewis and, with a single movement, he pulled Will's pants down to his ankles. Will jerked down to cover himself, momentarily slipping within Jimmy's grasp on his neck. He reached down in a futile attempt to pull up his pants and was kicked to the floor by Lewis. Lewis, a football player and weightlifter, grabbed Will by the arms and legs, raised him up above his head, pinned him against the roof of the bus, and held him there, sixty pounds of pale angularity against the yellow sheet metal. The bus swayed as it rounded the corner to Will's house. Will thought, *I've got to get off this bus. I can't stay on.* But he hung there, pinned against the riveted cool surface of the bus roof and a strange calm came over him. He glanced down at the faces of those watching below and found problems he would not solve for years. Jimmy's girl was flushed, her badly made-up eyes bright with excitement. Jimmy's eyes were averted, and a smirk of discomfort stained his lower face. Lewis gritted his teeth and grinned up at Will, mocking, and then he whispered something through unmoving lips, or was it just his foul breath? Will heard words like hot wind, *There's a meanness in this world.* A stench filled Will's nostrils, and he closed his eyes. He felt weak and sick to his stomach.

The bus slowed down, then stopped. Will saw his sisters rise from near the back of the bus, on opposite sides of the aisle, but they did not move toward the front.

*Falkes!* yelled the bus driver.

*Well, I guess if you're going to get off, I got to let you down*, said Lewis, with a smile.

Just before Lewis dropped him half-naked to the floor of the bus, Will glanced fully into Joyce Causey's eyes and found in their still darkness a pain he recognized.

It seemed to Will that he floated a long moment in the sunlit air of the bus before he crashed down onto the dusty, plate metal floor. He was unable to catch himself. He lay on his back, numb. He could not breathe. Out of a red haze, he heard his sister Barbara's voice from nearby, whispering, *For God's sake, Will, pull up your pants and get up! We're home.* Will struggled to his feet, pulled up his pants, and ran from the bus.

## SEVENTY-TWO

Nici watched her brother burst out of the bus and run to the garage. *Where was his book satchel?* As Will disappeared around the house, Barbara appeared in the bus door, dragging Will's satchel. She threw it from the door of the bus into the grass beside the road and turned back, grinning uneasily at the laughter she heard behind her on the bus. Then Judith pushed Barbara off the bus.

She barely escaped falling into the gravel road. She screamed at Judith, to the greater amusement of those on the bus.

Nici would fetch the satchel later, but now she looked toward the garage. Will ran from it with the puppy slung over his shoulder in a burlap bag. He tore blindly across the yard, through the gate and the garden, stumbling as he ran out past the barn toward the pond. When he reached the fence, he threw himself between two strands of barbed wire, catching his shirt and then tearing himself free with an awkward toss of his head and shoulders. The puppy yelped as the wire cut it.

Nici did not follow Will down to the pond as she usually did. She climbed the rough boards connecting the garage with the feed house and jumped onto the garage roof. She went to the crown of the roof and gazed at the pond. She resolved not to go in to supper until Will did—even if it meant Aunt Lennie's displeasure. Without knowing what happened on the bus, she sensed that it was bad. From where she was she saw Will come up out of the ditch before the pond. By a large rock there, she saw him raise the puppy up over his head.

Nici fell back on the roof and looked up into the bright blue sky.

When she rose up and looked for him again, she saw him below her, near the stump and among the nascent potato vines. He was digging at the edge of the garden with his hands. She rose and watched Will bury a burlap bundle in the soft soil of the first row of the potato patch.

That night she did not sleep for a long time, despite her sisters' unusual silence at bedtime.

## SEVENTY-THREE

That night after supper, Ray sat alone at the dinner table for a time. Nici, Judith, and Barbara had retreated to their room and were quiet. Lennie was reading to Will. Ray couldn't keep track of that boy. Once he went in his room, Ray let him be till morning—unless he cried out in the night. Ray was satisfied with Will recently. No complaints from school, and he did his chores. Will said he gave the dog away. That was that. The boy was all right or going to be all right. There was no substitute for discipline. Anytime that boy kept a dog in the past, it was trouble. He was always running off with the dog, playing instead of doing his work. Ray had enough of that.

He helped Lennie clear the table and wash the dishes. Then he watched as she made biscuits for breakfast. After she rolled them, he cut them, and she placed them in a pan. Then she covered them with a moist cloth, placed them in the refrigerator, said good night, and headed for the small room off the hallway where she settled those months ago with her single suitcase and straw hat. She came on a Greyhound, would leave on a Greyhound, and Ray would be sorry to see her go back to Hopkinsville. All childhood forgiven, she was the backbone of his life. She lent him the down payment for the farm and now she looked after his family for the long months since Ruth left and came back a ghost of herself.

After bidding his sister good night, he went in to read from *A Bowl of Brass* to Ruth. After a time, she dozed off in the rocker they moved into the corner of their bedroom. He gently picked up her frail form and carefully arranged her night garments as he placed her on the toilet. *Okay, Honey. You can go now.* Afterwards, he rearranged her garments and took her to bed in his tired arms as if she were a rag doll. As he laid her down, he thought he felt, yes, a slight pressure from her hand as it slipped from his neck. Had her hand clung to him, just a little? He studied her face, placid below her long ragged crew cut. He gently traced the deep indenture of the long, U-shaped scar in her scalp with his single forefinger, and then walked quietly to his dresser to empty his pockets and to account for his day.

*God, if you are there*, he prayed standing before the dresser, *bring her back. Please bring her back. If I'm never right about another thing, let her come back to me. I will never say another hurtful thing to her. I promise you. Just please bring her back to me. Take this great child from me and return my dear friend, my helpmate.*

## SEVENTY-FOUR

Will sat in a far corner of the library. He clutched the small book of verse, his eyes dancing over the pattern of lines on the page. Each line sang on the paper and interlocked with the following line, its sounds like music, whole words repeating, sounds flowing like wind and water. Will read the lines over and over, guessing at the words he did not know. Just their sound, their sound. *I caught this morning morning's minion*, he sang softly, his finger brushing each word as his breath shaped it. Then came the odd, bumpy part like stuttering—*dapple-dawn-drawn*—as if the speaker was struck dumb by the sight of the Falcon. *Like me*, Will thought, *he found Hawk.*

Then the magic began and Will read *in his riding of the rolling level underneath him steady air.* Yes, for Hawk the air was steady—like Lady's back when he rode her. Then the poet said exactly what Will felt when he watched Hawk: *My heart in hiding stirred.* Yes, stirred *for the mastery of the thing,* the bird, the Windhover, the Hawk.

And then the words streamed in a fiery row across the page to the best words of all, *here Buckle!* Will knew why those words were there. *Here* was the highest place, the best place—the tip of the pine, where Hawk cried out, *Here, here!* But it was also here inside him—*here Buckle! Here* was inside him, in his heart. And *Buckle.* Ah, such a beautiful word! It tied the lines, the poem together like a belt tightening around a waist.

Then another name for Hawk, *Chevalier.* He ran to the dictionary—*Prince*, it said—and sailed back to his corner of the library. Like *minion* earlier. Names for God, for Christ. God in nature, God in flight. Good. And *the fire that breaks from thee* is like lightning. Now put that inside and it is what? What is lightning inside? Lovely, dangerous. *A billion times more.* Will felt his heart racing loudly as he thought about it, about all the light, the lightning as thick as his body, sometimes as thick as the pine's trunk at the bottom, flowing from heaven to earth in streams of liquid fire. Only imagine this a million times bigger, the world full of exploding rivers of light! How beautiful.

Will said the next magic word, *sillion.* These new and strange and wonderful words, what did they mean? That word he did not find in the dictionary, but it must be earth or in the earth because a plow cuts it in the poem. Perhaps rich farm soil. *Gold-vermillion* was another mysterious word.

And what did it all mean? A mystery. The final name, *my dear.* That was love, not just for the bird—the flight. Then came Will's word, *fall.* Everything falls. The writer meant embers falling from burning wood. Does Hawk also fall from the burning sky? *Forced to fall by furious storm.* Yes, and lightning strikes the earth, the pine—*fire breaks* like love. That was it! The lightning inside is love. This poem is about love—love for Hawk, love for God. God was Hawk, or in Hawk, its flight. Fly and fall in lightning. All things.

Will stared blankly down at the page, his eyes useless. He closed the book and stared at the cover, with its golden cross on green. He would read this book, every word.

## SEVENTY-FIVE

Saint Andrew's Cathedral rang with festive sound on Easter Sunday. Will sat between his parents. Little Nici was in the nursery and Will's two older sisters nearby with their friends. Before them stood the Right Reverend Bishop Robert Brown, splendid in black and white robes, a brilliant strip of color draped over his broad shoulders.

*So infinitely far above,* Bishop Brown intoned.

Will's eyes swept from the richly decorated shoulders and silver coin spectacles of the bishop up to the vaulted roof and over the stained glass windows behind the altar, where the holy ghost was depicted as a white dove floating down in gold and ivory clouds.

*And so we come to this most sacred and mysterious of Holy Days, my friends, the day on which our beloved Savior was called up from death and rose to join his Father, shedding the last earthly bindings and bidding a brief farewell to his earthly followers.*

Will looked up at his father beside him, then down at his father's big square hands in which the hymnal had awkwardly lodged itself. He saw his father's eyes harden in recognition of his stare. Will glanced up at his mother, who slumped weakly beside him. Lennie's wary arm rested on the pew behind Ruth's shoulders. He looked again at the bishop, whose large hands now encircled the bejeweled cross on his chest. The bishop raised the cross and the light caught it.

*So great was his love for us that he gave his life for us, so that he might become our salvation. His arms were spread on a wooden cross and his hands pierced by nails. Through his suffering, his sacrifice for us—though we be heavy with sin—we can fly to him when we are called to eternity and rest in the fragrance of his arms.*

*We can fly like Hawk to him,* whispered Will.

*Sh-h-h-h!* his father hissed at him.

*So you see, my dear brothers and sisters, it is through His sacrifice that we attain eternal salvation. Through Him, we may experience the boundless love and eternal glory of God, when we are released from this flesh and rise to the stars, the rich o'rehanging firmament that is God's eternal home.*

The bishop placed the glittering cross back on his chest and clasped his hands out before him, shoulder high. The plane of his face rose, and Will smiled as he saw a red and gold swirl of sun-lit leaves around the bishop's face. Will stared at the stained glass dove behind and above the Bishop. The sound of wind filled his ears, and he began to imagine the flight of Hawk far above the earth.

*Let us today open our arms to those here beside us as Jesus our Savior opens his arms to us every moment of every day of our lives.*

A coolness swept over Will's body, and he crushed the open hymnal to his chest.

*Let us take this moment to rise and turn to those near us and offer them a hand, a kind word, an embrace. Surely we can bring God's work into our lives in this way. My dear friends, rise and greet each other in Christian love.*

Will rose with the congregation. His father shook hands with the man in the pew in front of them but did not turn in Will's direction. Will's mother did not rise; she appeared to be sleeping. Will saw two ushers embrace behind them. The cathedral was awash with murmurs and soft laughter. The congregation seated itself again as the bishop returned from the smiling embrace of the Canon to the pulpit and looked with clear eyes out over the congregation. His arms rose, opening wings of white, as if to enclose them all.

*Oh, my dear brothers and sisters, don't you know how much God loves you?*

The bishop remained with his arms outstretched for a long moment, then let them fall silently to his sides and turned to face the altar. Will felt his heart fly up and circle high above him in the ornamental lights of the cathedral. The organ intoned the opening phrase of the offertory hymn. As he and his father rose with the congregation, Will grasped his father's hand and drew it to his chest. Ray's hymnal crashed to the floor. His eyes glared questioningly at Will above an embarrassed grimace.

*Will?* he uttered. His eyes were dark and angry.

The hymn began. Ray struggled to free his hand. The congregation sang strongly.

*A mighty fortress is our god,*
*A bulwark never failing.*
*Our helper he, amid the flood*
*Of mortal ills prevailing.*

Will looked into this father's eyes, and clung to his hand. Ray bent over Will, threatening him with his voice. *Will, stop it!*

The congregation continued:

*For still our ancient foe*
*Does seek to work us woe;*

Will released the hand and stood frozen as he watched his

father retrieve his hymnal. Ray glanced down on Will red-faced, fumbled for his place, and rejoined the congregation for the final phrases in his rough, out of tune voice.

*And armed with cruel fate*
*On earth is not his equal.*

Will stared at the floor. The heavy offertory plate passed by him. The final prayers sounded, distant. The recessional moved in a stately fashion down the aisle and out into the vestibule where it formed a milling, joyful crowd.

## SEVENTY-SIX

Will passed through the heavy wooden doors in a cloud of dizziness, ran around the corner of the church, and ducked into the shaggy evergreen shrubbery enclosing the skirts of the edifice. The memory of the recessional clouded his thoughts, hiding the blinding nausea he felt. He sank down on his knees. As he did whenever something dreadful came at him, he looked around for something to draw him from the reality approaching like the monstrous sting of the razor strap. He was surrounded by a haze of fragrant green, except for the chunks of natural stone that formed the wall of the church. He studied the glimmering, rough surface of the heavy rock, felt the violent surge of everything within him suddenly leave. He sank back, hugged his knees, and let the tears come. Little by little, he began to breathe more easily. He heard the people chattering happily as they exited the service, and now and then through the haze of sound and light beginning to filter through the fir shrubs, he heard the bishop's voice calling out greetings to his flock. When the bishop said, *My dear brothers and sisters, Don't you know how much God loves you?* Will felt a chill run through him, and he wanted to run to the Bishop and fill his robed arms. But instead he turned to his father, whose arms opened for firewood, fence posts, tomato sticks, even rolls of barbed wire, but not for his son. *Not for me*, Will thought.

People embraced in the Bible. Fathers embraced sons, sometimes. The Old Testament was full of wonderful stories, but they were not stories of sweet, kind love, like his mother's or Tyree's. They were full of the opposite—pain and loneliness and terror. In the first story about people, there was a couple, Adam and Eve, like his mother and father, They were happy and innocent, but then the snake came and they were driven out of the garden. If God loved them, why did this happen? Maybe love didn't always mean being happy. *God is love*, his Sunday school teachers said over and over, but in some of the old stories God cursed people and tried to kill them—all of them. When God spoke like this in the old stories, Will heard the voice of those around him who hated others, like the children at school who told such mean jokes about others or said such mean things about black folk or those other people Will had so many questions about—the Jews. Who were they really? Who was Mr. Gold? Why did people say such mean things about them, even the preachers at revivals? And if God was love, why did people on earth kill him? Why was he forced to give his life? Why were Adam and Abraham and Jesus so unhappy if God is love? God was their father. Maybe the problem is with them, not God. Why didn't their father love them? Maybe the same reason his father didn't love him. Maybe his father's love was like God's love, hard and cold and full of tests. He lay back on the warm earth, lost in thought. The sunlight filtered through the evergreen canopy above him. There was, somehow, so much beauty—Hawk's flight, his great pine, Mr. Gold's arias, chess, Tyree, his mother—in the world.

Will's favorite story was of Abraham greeting the three strangers. Does he know they are angels, messengers of God, when he greets them? He invites them to join him in the shade of his trees, like Mr. Chambers and Will sat in the persimmon orchard together after gathering fruit, and Ty and he sat in the grove where the well was. Abraham feeds them, washes their feet—probably sore from walking. Was that love? When he read that story, it seemed like love to him. Abraham washes their feet. His mother used to wash him, and he loved that. Yes, that was love. Surely every mother bathed her child and the child loved it. In the revival tent, the people knelt in the narrow pews and washed their neighbor's feet. That looked so beautiful. Surely that was love. To be like Abraham and treat a stranger like a messenger from God. Then shouldn't family and close neighbors, like Tyree and Mr. Chambers, be loved even more? Yet people who had been neighbors for a long time hated each other. How could that be? Why did a white person hate a black person, a Christian hate a Jew? Strange, to love hate instead of love. Maybe fathers were not meant to touch and hug their children. Maybe they just fed them. Maybe that was enough.

He crawled from under the evergreens and saw his mother tottering, clinging to Ray's arm. She glanced tiredly around the churchyard, her forehead marred by slight wrinkles. In that moment he felt that this woman was his mother again. In a blink, he flew across the lawn and was in her arms—before she could utter a word of worried love, before his nearby father could utter a curse. He was in her frail arms and safe though swaying for a short but endless time.

## SEVENTY-SEVEN

Mr. Gold's head rose from the book he was reading and he leaned back against the heavy bookcase. He and Will sat on the floor in a dim aisle of the Monticello Library, surrounded by small piles of books. It was one of their Saturday afternoons in the library. They met there sometimes on Saturdays since first listening to music together in Mr. Gold's apartment.

Will felt Mr. Gold's eyes on him, and his eyes rose to meet them.

*Will, how old are you?* Mr. Gold whispered.

*I was seven on February 13.*

*Seven, hum?* he asked. *I have told you that you remind me of someone I knew once.*

*Yes, I remember.*

*A little boy I lost.* He sighed. *He was very bright, like you, and he too loved music.*

*My mother sings*, said Will, simply.

*Ah, then*, murmured the old man, smiling. *This explains it all. You love it when your mother sings?*

Will did not know what to say, so he nodded. Then he added, *And she says her cousin is a great singer. I don't know him.*

*Yes, that's good. You come from a musical family, a family of singers*, said Mr. Gold. *My mother also sang. I remember she sang me to sleep.*

Will nodded again. *And when I wake up in the night, she sings again.*

*You wake in the night?*

*Bad dreams.*

*Ah, yes*, and now Mr. Gold nodded. *Me, too.*

Will was surprised, sat up straight. *You, too?*

*Oh, yes, my dear Will.*

Will was overcome with a strange recognition. *What are yours about?*

Mr. Gold's eyebrows raised suddenly. He slumped back heavily against the bookshelf and closed his eyes.

Will did not know to take back his question. He stared cross-eyed and pure at Mr. Gold, and the old man knew the pain of the world in those eyes.

*I dream about a little boy, like you, and his mother.* His hands dropped, and he swayed forward in an odd rhythm of his upper body. *And I dream of my mother's voice.* His slender body began to shake like a young tree in the wind.

Will was frightened of things he knew he could not understand. He did nothing.

Mr. Gold stilled himself and looked deeply into Will's eyes.

*It is good, Will. We are friends. And friends can talk of such things, can't they? Of course, they can. That is what friends do.*

Will found himself in the old man's arms and was happy there, encased as he was in the pleasant aura of wool tweed, camphor, and cigarette ash that was Mr. Gold. Then Will remembered the word he saved for Mr. Gold.

*Mr. Gold*, said Will, wriggling deeper into Mr. Gold's slight arms.

*Yes, Will*, the old man said.

*What is vermilion?* Will had saved the word for Mr. Gold because *Gold-vermilion* was the word in the poem. It seemed to call for Mr. Gold's help.

*Vermilion, the color?* Mr. Gold shook his head in confused wonder at Will's leap. Somehow, for him, a connection. What could he do? *Yes, an unusual color. A deep reddish orange, I think. Where do we find it? In the sunset, after rain; in dying embers; in wet clay, the kind Adam was shaped from.*

Will breathed a soft word and was asleep.

*Dream*, the old man thought as he held the boy. *Ether haunts you and another gas haunts me. Those who breathe your gas wake up to dream again; you wake to breathe again, dear boy. My little one did not wake up.*

## SEVENTY-EIGHT

Ruth lay on the couch in the living room and looked up at her son. Her head rested on a pillow on his lap. She watched delightedly as her Will sang to her. His voice was pure and warm, but not childlike. Yet it was his. On the chorus of this haunting little song, she hummed along. *Dona, dona, dona.* Her voice was rough, deep in her throat. Still, it felt good to hum.

When he finished, she said, *Again.* And he sang it again.

> *On a wagon bound for market*
> *There's a calf with a mournful eye.*
> *High above it, there's a swallow,*
> *Winging swiftly through the sky.*

His voice was silk, warm like sun. The scene was beautiful—a calf, a bird, bouncing down a country road. *Dona, dona, dona.* Lovely.

> *Stop complaining, said the farmer,*
> *Who told you a calf to be.*
> *Why don't you have wings to fly with*
> *Like the swallow so proud and free?*

*The calf must have been lowing, or crying out,* thought Ruth. *The farmer sounds mean. Poor calf, away from its mother. Why should it fly like the swallow?* She stopped humming and studied her son's beautiful face, its glowing pink cheeks, the fine dark-blond hair lying on his high forehead, the bright sky of his eyes. She reached out and brushed a strand of hair lightly, and then her hand fell away.

In another moment, Will saw that his mother was asleep, but he finished the little song Mr. Gold taught him.

> *Calves are easily bound and slaughtered,*
> *Never knowing the reason why.*
> *But whoever savors freedom,*
> *Like the swallow, has learned to fly.*
>
> *How the winds are laughing,*
> *They laugh with all their might,*
> *Laugh and laugh the whole day through*
> *And half the summer's night.*
>
> *Dona, dona, dona.*

It seemed to Will, if there were a heaven, it would be like this—his mother asleep in his arms.

Listening in the next room, Lennie sat in Ruth's rocker and crocheted a tulle for Ruth. When it was finished, she would leave. It was time for Ruth to get up. Her old friend was gone and buried deep inside this one, and a new one had to be born somehow. Lennie celebrated the tears on her face. She had not cried since little Fred died. Fifteen years. Will's voice moaned sweetly in the next room, flowed through her like a visitation of the afterlife, and she slowly, cautiously let the mystery of love fill her.

#### SEVENTY-NINE

Late rains delayed some of the spring planting. Will worked hard at everything Ray gave him. No words passed between them except instructions. He gave single word answers to his father's questions about school. They planted and hoed for long, silent hours evenings and weekends. When school was out, Will would work entire days. No matter how much Will did, Ray found more for him to do. And for once, it seemed to Ray, Will accepted what his father asked of him. Yet he was somehow, Ray felt, removed— like Ruth, like his mother. After planting, they'd be back at work on the house.

*Where is that boy?* Ray thought more than once. *Well, as long as he does the work.*

In late spring, Ray often went into the potato patch with his hoe. The tendrils were now dark green and beginning to search out their paths. He studied the way the vines spread, clinging to the earth; he knew that the roots spread out similarly under the soil's surface, like a shadow of what he saw. Ray thought ahead to harvest, his favorite time of year, as he cut the weeds among the vines and loosened the soil wherever there was space enough. There was something about potato digging that Ray found peaceful. In fall, he bent and discovered the clotted tubers deep in the loose dark soil, each tuber connected to the roots by febrile strands. Later, he washed each potato and let it dry in the air. They kept for weeks, sometimes months in the dry feed house.

Then there was the cakey soil itself. It was dark and rich behind the house west of the stump. Perhaps that area had all been forest once. He worked rhythmically till he was near the stump; then he saw a piece of burlap extending out of the soil. His searching hand grasped it and pulled the bag from the earth. There was something in it, something so unexpected that his curiosity turned back to the dark beside his childhood door.

Ruth sat sleeping, the afternoon light on her face, when she was stirred from a vague dream by the back screen door's sound. Returning reluctantly to the cottony dream that was her waking life, she listened carefully for clues. It was an old tactic necessitated on some level by living her whole life with families turgid with secret fears. She heard Ray speaking loudly to himself—as he did only when he was upset. Lennie was at a church picnic, she remembered; the children were at school. She and Ray were alone, as at the beginning.

Then Ray was there before her, his face ashen. His hands were clotted with moist earth and he clasped something in his hand, a sack. *Why were his brogans still on*, Ruth wondered? *Dirt would be everywhere. And what was that dreadful smell?*

A pain entered her mind then breast like a vast needle piercing her from above, and she began to see the necessity of returning to this needful man and his children.

### EIGHTY

As he lighted from the school bus, Will heard Ray's howl and knew he had found the buried sack. Will knew this moment would come even when he buried it.

Then Will was running wide around the house, climbing or hurtling fences, making his way toward a safe place, high in the corner of the cornfield. His father could follow him there but not climb after him. *If I make it to the pine, I will be safe up there. I will be near Hawk.*

As he reached the tree, Will heard his father's scream and looked over his shoulder. He saw his father striding out after him, a double bit axe clutched at the end of his arm. Will ran up to the pine, grasped its rough skin and scampered up to the first large limb. The tree was already alive with wind and as Will swung up to the next limb, the fibrous mass of the pine was murmuring something sinewy and vague to him. He ascended, mounting each rung of the rough ladder leading him up into the narrowing wind to the towering pine's apex and away from the danger below. There he clung and looked for the wings of Hawk and above that, the wings of the storm he saw approaching from out over Tyree's place. Soon the wind was full upon him, beginning to work its will on the vast rippling surface far below.

## EIGHTY-ONE

Tyree stopped hoeing in his vegetable garden and looked up into the heavens. He had never seen clouds like those boiling in the sky above the Falke place. They swelled up above the forested horizon like vast malignant toadstools threatening to erupt. Then he thought he heard Will's voice, a part of the wind at first, then bright and crying out like a bird.

*Pa!* Joshua called out from the front porch. Tyree turned to see his son gazing toward the Falke place. He could see the top of the pine, and Will was in it. Tyree dropped his hoe, crossed past his house and wagon and went down the path that led from his house onto the Falke's place. He walked quickly—with apprehension. He hadn't seen Will in the better part of a month, since the dance on the wagon, and he was in his own way worried about the boy. He assumed that the puppy had returned to the Falke place, but he was busy over at Burke's and hadn't looked into it. At the frail wire fence separating the properties, he paused and listened. There were only the trees lashing violently above him and above that the boiling gray sky. He pulled apart the loose strands of barbed wire and crossed between them onto Falke property.

As Tyree approached the field behind the pine, the trees opened on a panorama. A powerful wind swept eastward, over his right shoulder, and it bent the trees and bushes before it. The grass was swept out before him like the surface of a vast ocean. Small dust clouds appeared, swirled violently, and disappeared as they had come. Above him, rows of clouds swept quickly toward where he knew the sun rose. It wasn't tornado weather, but it was bad a real thunderstorm. Heaven's gonna meet the earth today.

Then he heard Will's voice up high, and, shielding his eyes against the wind, he saw the boy seventy, maybe eighty feet up near the top of the old pine, clinging to the tree's uppermost part. The treetop was leaning heavily to one side in the wind, then snapping back violently.

*Will!* The name escaped his lips and in that moment he knew how much the boy meant to him. He ran toward the tree waving his arms—at what he did not know, but his heart yelled out, *Come down, Will Honey. Come back on down to earth. You just the boy to think he can fly, but my God you can't. Come down here to old Tyree!*

Overcome by love as he was, he was stopped short by what he saw beneath the tree.

## EIGHTY-TWO

In his mind, Ray moved heavily across the early spring furrows toward the pine. He had no sense of the mad stamping of his legs through the broken soil, as if they were possessed by a fury pure and terrible. He saw the small figure he pursued reach the tree and scamper ten feet up the thick trunk to the first branches, then disappear into the thick cone of the tree's body. He saw his son escape upward, into a place he knew he could not go. He lurched forward into a run and then tripped and fell heavily onto the flat of the axe. He had not known he had it, but he gripped it ever tighter as he sprang to his feet. He heard a familiar voice of warning as he rose, but mistaking it for a drunken voice from the dark mirror of his past, he ignored it and moved up to the tree.

He never knew what he cried up into that tree. He did not know how often he struck the tree in wildness. So far was he from himself that if lightning had risen from his raised axe to the heavens and burned his ecstasy from him, he would have crumbled indifferent to the love of his family for him. Had he seen the gaunt form of his father—when sober the kindest, gentlest man in the county; when drunk, the meanest—emerge from the trunk of the pine, he could not have stopped, so far had his passion torn him from himself.

*Who determines who lives and dies?* He screamed up into the tree. *How dare you live? You were not the first-born. What right have you to kill? What right have you to live? I hate you, I hate you, I hate you.*

Then someone cried out his name—not Ray, but a familiar old name. He whirled and the night wind became his mirror and he saw his brother Faye before him in his father's arms and his father was crying and singing an old song and rocking his little blond brother in his arms. *Faye*, he cried out, and fell back on the broken earth.

Then the voice was upon him and he knew whose it was and knew that he had to listen to it or be damned. It was the voice of all he knew as good. He fell and listened to it and, as he listened, it was as if heavy, foul scales fell from him, fell jeweled into the earth he had torn open with fierce labor.

## EIGHTY-THREE

*Ted, we both know our father was what he was.*
*His life was hard and yours hasn't been easy either,*
   *but Ted you have no call to do this.*
*This boy has never hurt you.*
*He's a good boy and he has his own grief.*
*You are not yourself,*
*You are outside yourself right now,*
*And you must listen to me.*
*You are my brother, my only brother,*
*but you must stop this.*
*If you hurt this boy, I'll have the law on you.*
*I will, Ted. I'll have the law on you like maybe*
*I should have had the law on your father*
   *when he did what he did.*
*But he was all we had, he was our law—*
*Still, you can't go on like this.*
*Don't summon death, Ted.*
*He'll come in his own good time.*
*That's your son up there and that's it.*
*He's yours, and Ruth's, and mine, and he's a good boy.*
*I've cooked for him and mended his shirts.*
*I've seen him with Nici and I've seen him with Ruth.*
*You have no reason for this.*
*You and he need time.*
*You can't kill our father, Ted—*
*He's dead twenty years, no matter what you feel.*
*There's no bringing him back to talk it out.*

*Let the fury go, Ted.*
*Let it become something else,*
   *like in the old stories.*
*Let it go under the earth*
   *and become a comfort.*
*Let go of it now, or I'll take your son away from you.*
*I'll take him and I'll go. And I'll never come back*
   *and you can face this pain alone.*
*Do you hear me, Ted? Do you?*
*I raised you and I tell you*
*You can't have this boy. You can't, I won't have it.*
*Now you come in out of this storm and leave the boy in peace.*

## EIGHTY-FOUR

Tyree watched Ray strike at the tree wildly with a big axe. Tyree could smell fury from the man there in the distance. It was a smell he often smelled in his own life, and he choked it back often enough—as had his father and grandfather. He jerked forward, but stopped as a tall, gaunt woman—Ray's sister, Tyree knew approached Ray and stood near him. At first, she grimly watched his wild dance as he hacked at the tree. She also looked up into the tree with a furrowed brow for Will. When she found him atop the tree, her face settled into a taut smile. Then Tyree heard her voice, strong as if she were standing next to him.

She cried out a name, a short name he had not heard before, and he watched the man pause with the axe high above his head. As if struck from behind on a field of battle, he whirled ready to strike his enemy. As he turned, axe high above him in mid-stroke, the woman quickly advanced on him until she stood directly before him. Then she spoke slowly and steadily at him, in phrases she punctuated by leaning in as if daring him to strike.

Without warning, as if struck by lightning, the man fell backwards, away from his sister, and the axe flew out of his hands. He fell on his back in the muddy field, his face in his hands. His sister stood over him and went on talking.

Tyree looked up and studied Will, who was—it seemed to the heavy man standing far below—moving now as a part of the tree in the flooding wind. As he watched, full of wonder, the boy opened his arms and called out in a high musical plaint that entered the wind's howl and somehow made it beautiful.

Tyree watched this strange tableau resolve its awful symmetry. Now the woman was kneeling beside the man, who cried curled up on the broken earth of the field. Exactly how long this continued, Tyree wasn't sure, but the cold violence of the rain was soon on him and the others and on Will. Long after the man and woman moved from the tree, Tyree watched as Will rode the wind, as alone as a child caught high in a rainstorm can be.

## EIGHTY-FIVE

Thunderstorm! Will clung to the thin crusty pole that was the pine at its top and felt the wind press against the immense cone of the tree spreading out beneath him like a whirlwind. At the edge of it stood his father, howling out something about hell, and the wind filled Will's ears, and he saw vast wings of clouds spread to the north and south, and he saw above him a great skull and beak and eyes opening slowly and the great spinning within the whorling sockets, then the bright reddish-gold of lightning, the bolt as thick as his own body, with the sharp smell filling the air about him, and the following great buckle of the air as the beak opened wide to him and as the wings swept by, and he and the tree bent far back as one and the boy cried out into the wind now filling his open mouth and the roiling air tossing his hair and pine bristles, his arms and pine limbs and all mixing as the smell of burnt pine and lightning and fear and pleasure filled his senses and drowned out his father and all the voices within him and in the world far below, and he moved silently in the crush of noise and motion toward his soul.

### EIGHTY-SIX

Will left his perch after the storm subsided and the west wind began to chill him painfully. He found Tyree at the bottom of the tree. Will refused sanctuary at Tyree's house and watched his huge friend move toward home through the brush. He seemed to the boy a great and mysterious figure who would never hide away when Will searched for him. Had he moved with vast wings across the surface of the wind-swept landscape, he could not have been more beautiful to Will.

Returning to the house, Will slipped barefoot into his parents' bedroom. He paused by the door, breathless with purpose. His hand lingered on the cool doorknob. He faintly heard his father and Lennie speaking in the kitchen. The room seemed a foreign country in its moonlit stillness. Lennie's star quilt was turned back on the right side of the bed, his mother's side, so that the corner intersected with the central figure of the many-colored star. The air was crisp, he could see his breath, and he knew in seeing the ephemeral cloud linger in the darkness why he had come. He had nowhere else to go. He slid down to a crouch on the floor, his back pressed against the wall beside the door. He still felt the cool wind from the pine's heights in his hair. His head leaned against his father's chest of drawers—he heard his father repeat the word *cursed*.

Will thought he could help somehow. Something had to happen—he had no idea what. He would make his stand here. Things could not go on as they were—he would rather fall endlessly, in his worst dream.

He heard his father's heavy steps in the hallway. His determination fled. Will glanced at the closet door fifteen feet away, then threw himself on the floor beside the bed and slithered under it. He was surprised at how much space existed between the fine wood floor he and his father had laid and the rusty springs of the bed. The oak floor was to Will strangely warm and yet he began to shiver soundlessly as he lay back on its even surface. At the foot of the bed was the cedar trunk whose fragrance filled his nostrils. His father made that for his mother, early in their marriage.

Ray's heavy tread approached the door. He was carrying Ruth, who must be exhausted or asleep. The bedroom door opened, then closed. Will watched his father's feet shuffle toward the bed; then the springs sank down a little toward Will. Will reached up and felt the cold wire frame above him. His father spoke.

*Ruth, I need to talk to you. You know I can't understand what you've been through, or know exactly how you feel now. But it seems you're better. Maybe a little?* His father's feet shifted beside the bed, then drifted over by the window. *I don't expect much.*

His mother murmured something very softly. Then, silence.

*Ruth*, his father continued, *Lennie wants to go back to Hopkinsville and get on with her life. She's been here the better part of a year.* His father's voice choked up in a way Will had never heard. *Ruth, it's been a long time.* His father's shoes returned to the bed from the window. They stopped beside the bed, inches from Will's hand. Will stopped himself from reaching out to them. *I need for you to come back, Ruth. Please. I can't do this alone. Please come back.* Ray sighed deeply and his shoes moved away from the bed and toward the door to the hallway. *I'll be back in a minute.* He paused a long time at the open door. *That's it; that's what I wanted to say to you.* And the door closed.

The room's stillness flooded over Will as his father's footsteps retreated down the hall. Then his mother shifted slightly in the bed above him, and he heard her sigh and begin to cry softly. Why he did what he did then, Will would never know, but it was for his boy's soul an act of undeclared love. He heard his voice humming before he knew it was to be. It was soft as a spider's web, and the melody was one Ruth had often sung to him. As it spun out of his darkness under the bed into the room's lunar stillness, Ruth's crying ceased. Will felt a warm chill run through him as he heard his mother's voice murmuring, *Will, is that you?*

He wasn't sure whether those words were shaped or merely unspoken song, but he cried out softly in that moment of his mother's utterance. His mother's hand appeared beside the bed, and he took it in his, and the slender pale coolness of it was a beauty he had sensed only in visions. Then the words came to him—*Alma*, the soul, the beautiful clinging sound of the voice in flight, the hawk in flight, the freedom atop things before the fall. Beauty flooded his heart. Could he have held that moment forever, he would have been the happiest of boys.

Ray left his brogans by the back doorstep and returned to his wife in his socks. In the hallway, he was stunned when he heard a whispering song inside his bedroom. It was one of Ruth's melodies, but not her voice. It was no louder than a gnat's whine. *Will was in there! What right did he have to be there, with her?* He turned, lost suddenly in the wilderness of his past, lost in the scattered dreams within him. The skin of his back and head burned, and his head spun. *Damn you, Father*, a voice within him cried out, and he hurtled toward the door, as if struck from behind by a great belt.

Before Will could catch his breath, the door burst open, and his father was in the room, dragging him out from under the bed by one hand and one foot. Will clung to the springs with one hand and blanked out the terrible hoarse question that filled the suddenly dark room.

Will's singing was echoing softly in Ruth's mind when her son's scalding hand entered hers. A split second later, the door crashed open and Ray burst into the room, shouting. He fell to his knees beside the bed. Ruth felt the bed begin to shudder violently beneath her. She struggled to sit up and to her surprise found that the jerking of the bed aided her. She worked her shoulders up the headboard until she could see the foot of the bed.

Ruth saw Will pulled from under the bed, one hand and one foot held in Ray's hands. Then, in an exercise of impossible strength, she saw Will tear himself free of Ray, strike his father in the face, leap over him, and run into the hall. Ray froze a moment on the floor, and in that moment his eyes met Ruth's. There was in his eyes something completely beyond her ken. A chill tore through her as she was struck by how much this man had changed since he whispered to her a few moments ago. How could such change occur? Who was this man?

As Ray rose slowly and stiffly, something in his stance frightened Ruth. As he moved toward the door, there was a simian grace to him. She saw the killer he could be, and as he moved into the hallway after Will, a thought ran through her like chill frost. *Will has no safe place.*

Ruth somehow threw her body toward the edge of the bed. As she found herself perched unsteadily there, an overwhelming force bent her forward. She cried to her husband as she had never been able to before. As she slid from the bed, she caught herself on wooden legs, and, leaning against the bed to steady her body, began to move unsteadily toward the door to the hallway.

Then Ruth heard Will cry out.

### EIGHTY-SEVEN

Ray's incomplete hands slipped off Will's extremities. The unexpectedness of the fall back onto the floor broke the ecstasy of his anger. As he rose to grab Will again, his son struck him full in the face with his tiny fist, a slight branch striking a running bear. Yet Ray fell back in shock. He felt a blunt pain, not in his face but in his chest. As he hesitated that instant, his eyes met Ruth's, and he could not breathe. She perched awkwardly on the bed like a great nestling, mouth agape, begging for food. He flashed on the first time he had ever bared his soul to Ruth, the moment of his question to her, the enormity of his risk and the terror he felt at her long moment's hesitation. He was tied to that moment by the slenderest of threads, the threads that attempted to hold him back now.

Still, he got quickly to his feet, determined not to be excelled by the little ape he had sired. He grasped the doorframe before following the fleeting shadow of his son down the hallway. He was no longer young, and the absurdity of his rage struck him. *You have fallen*, a slight voice far back within him said, and wisdom crushed him beneath it in that moment, *now listen and watch for signs. Wait and watch. Do not rush from this place to the unknown.* Whose voice was it—Lennie's? Faye's?

He saw the pale angles of his son's form brush against the wall running blindly down the hall, then hover frozen on one foot for a moment over the small rough mound that he knew to be a nail sack. Then Will's cry pierced Ray's heart as nothing ever had, and the force of its pain crashed into his plummeting rage. As he entered the hallway, he heard a sound that he had longed for these many months. His wife's voice, hoarse and high, called out the admonition of his life.

*Ray, no!*

Ray hesitated just inside the hall door as his wife's voice seared into him, further severing the power of his ancient need to hate. In that second hesitation, he saw Will's flight down the hallway broken. The boy fell against the wall and then lurched into his room on one foot.

As Ray moved down the hallway, nails caught under his feet, then skittered across the hardwood floor. *That will scar the surface*, he grimaced. He heard his son's high whine from within his room.

Sure of nothing, Ray hesitated before the door, studying the moon's light on the new paint—Will painted it himself on the doorframe. It seemed ivory as he moved through it.

Ray expected to find Will cowering at the window or under the covers, but the boy was on his narrow bed, curled up on his back, his slender, bare foot held high by both hands at the ankle. Two sixteen-penny nails were in the foot—one pierced the sole and emerged point up from the top, a second buried itself half way up in the heel. Will's head was back, his teeth clinched, and a high whine emerged from his barely parted lips. Then his eyes locked his father's, and the whining transformed itself to a slight whimper.

Ray moved, unhesitating, toward his son.

Later, Ruth could not explain how she moved to the bedroom door. She was at the bed on dead legs, then at the door. She seemed at first to be waiting in a vast yard for something unspeakable to happen. It was a thing she did not want to see, but she had no choice. She could not move, yet she had to. These men were hers. The slight hand of her son still burned in hers, echoing in her senses.

As she clung to the doorjamb, a stinging pain like childbirth coursed through her lower body. She saw her husband emerge from Will's room, a bundle in his arms. As Ray walked the three steps toward her that measured the distance from Will's bedroom to the bathroom, she glimpsed a certain light about his eyes. He entered the bathroom and Will's whimpering was drowned out by running water and the slight but penetrating scream of the hot water faucet.

The clock in their room rang out ten softly. At the opposite end of the dark hallway, she saw the pale orbs of her two older daughters' faces staring at her. She felt little Nici's arms around her knees, and then she collapsed into Lennie's strong arms. She managed a whisper to her sister-in-law as she was firmly tucked into bed.

*Check on Will, please. He's with Ray.*

Lennie gazed into the bathroom and saw her hopes realized. Ray was on his knees, his left arm supporting Will's slumping form on the tub's edge. Ray's right hand gently washed his son's pierced foot in the shallow water of the tub. Will seemed to be whispering to his father and Ray nodded in response. The two nails lay on the floor beside the tub.

*Do you need help, Ray?* she asked.

The eyes her brother raised to her were those of the injured boy who returned from a flooded stream that spring day, all hope crushed. They were eyes that said *no* and, at the same time, *Please God yes*. They were the eyes of their own father in the final days of his life, his gangrenous leg poisoning all his gaunt body. It was surrender to a higher thing than he had ever known. To find love in that great pain, Lennie said to herself, was truly a blessing.

Lennie counted all her blessings for the next half-hour, during which she put the three girls back to bed and swept the hall. As Will eased from shock toward sleep, she took the boy from her brother's arms and carried him to his little room. She bathed the entrance and exit wounds with iodine and bound them loosely. There would be tetanus shots the next morning. She would see to it.

When she finished, she returned to the bathroom and found her brother slumped on the floor by the tub. His unseeing eyes were open and yet he seemed asleep. She thought him dead for a moment, then heard his slow, measured breathing. She crossed to him, went on one knee beside him, and for the first time either could remember, she touched him gently on the shoulder.

*Ray, I'm tired. I'm going to bed now.*

He turned his eyes to look at her, and she was convinced of her reward, her wages of the soul. And she helped him raise himself upright before she left him at the window studying his land with its fences and moonlit forms.

## EIGHTY-EIGHT

Several days later, Ray strode out of the woods into the clearing and toward the unpainted sharecropper house. Tyree sat on the front porch with his boy beside him, whittling. Ray whistled a short birdsong and Tyree raised his eyes. He did not rise to greet Ray, nor did he extend his hand. Ray walked directly up to him and held out the leather bag Lennie found at the well. Tyree studied the bag distantly.

*This is yours*, Ray said.

Tyree shook his head no, his dark eyes locked on Ray's blue.

*My sister said it was. She saw you and the boy play in the draw.*

*Sure, we played*, said Tyree. *But they ain't mine no more. They Mr. Will's. He won them fair and square.* Tyree smoothed the rim of his felt hat and smiled. *And he won more than that.*

*You taught him to play chess?* Ray's voice was even and controlled.

*That boy quick. It wasn't no big thing.*

*It was to him*, Ray said. He studied the sag in the shack's roof. *He taught my sister to play.*

*Miss Lennie? He done that? My, my, what all that boy up to.*

*You know*, said Ray, measured, *I could help you brace that porch roof.* And he moved his hand in a line parallel to the imaginary beam of repair.

Tyree leaned back and studied the roof's sag, then said slowly, *No, Sir. That old roof, he just fine like he is.* He looked at Ray directly, in recognition of his offer. *But I thank you, sir. I do.* A long moment passed, and both men were fine with it. *And you tell old Will those pieces are for him.* Tyree whittled them from pine and oak for him.

*I can pay you for them*, offered Ray.

*Oh no*, murmured Tyree. *Mr. Will done all that.* Then he said, brightly, *Don't you know, he helped me dig that old hole in the ground?*

*I saw him down there with you*, said Ray.

*Yeh*, said Tyree, shaking his head at the memory. *That boy work free.*

*That will change, Tyree*, said Ray, grimly.

*I don't think so. I truly do not*, said Tyree.

And the two men studied each other.

Ray opened the bag and took out some pieces. He took the dark horse and examined it closely, then smelled it. *Berry? I have some wood stain in my garage. You're welcome to it.*

Tyree stood up. *I have my ways already. But I thank you. I thank you for Will.*

Ray's eyes met Tyree's. *It's there if you want it.* Ray turned to go, but stopped. *And I thank you, Tyree*, he said, his eyes searching the ground at this feet.

*You welcome, Mr. Falke*, said Tyree.

Ray raised his right palm in a brief gesture of farewell. Then he was stealing away, as he had come, moving back through the woods on the path of Tyree's epiphany that stormy day.

As his own hand moved gently over the curve of his son Joshua's head, Tyree's heart sang an old, sweet song that mixed pain and joy into a final thing that he could live with.

### EIGHTY-NINE

The boy followed the arcing flight of the swept form far above him and when it flew into the dark circle of the wing-brushed sun, he did not flinch at the blinding pain but extended both his arms to it and felt his body rise to one leg, then somehow farther upward. Will's gesture flew to his watching father and pierced that heart with healing. Ray glimpsed an austere beauty in his son's face. And from the distance between them marked by the oak posts and barbed wire of their time together thus far, each knew the other as much as was allowed their willing hearts.

Will turned to the house and saw his father. Behind him and before the rough beauty of the partially restored house, he saw his mother, standing slight and pale as an ivory trellis. He turned back to Hawk and the river of clouds flowing swiftly above it.

Ruth watched her men from the porch steps, grasped them anew, and caught their image in the slender book of her memory.

William Wallis was raised in the South. His *Selected Poems 1969-99* was nominated for the Pulitzer Prize. He resides in Los Angeles. *Hawk* is his first novel.

## Also by William Wallis

**POETRY**
*Poems*
*Biographer's Notes*
*Four Valley Poets* (with others)*
*Ruth**
*Asher**
*Eros*
*Dutton's Books**
*Joshua**
*Twins*
*Simple Gifts**
*Selected Poems**

**PROSE**
*A Meeting of Cultures*
Essays on Lakota History and Culture, Literature and Music

*Selected Essays**

*A Dream of Love Fulfilled**
An Introduction to Romantic Opera as Literature

**DRAMA**
*Hanblecheya, The Vision*

## Edited by William Wallis

*Dream Songs**
Poetry by Giti Moghimi

*Traveling Inland**
Poetry by Flora Wallis Foss

*Marty, A Boy From Brooklyn*
by Martin R. Horn

## Forthcoming

*Nebraska Symphony*
The Story of Charles Leonard Thiessen

*Available from Stone and Scott, *Publishers*